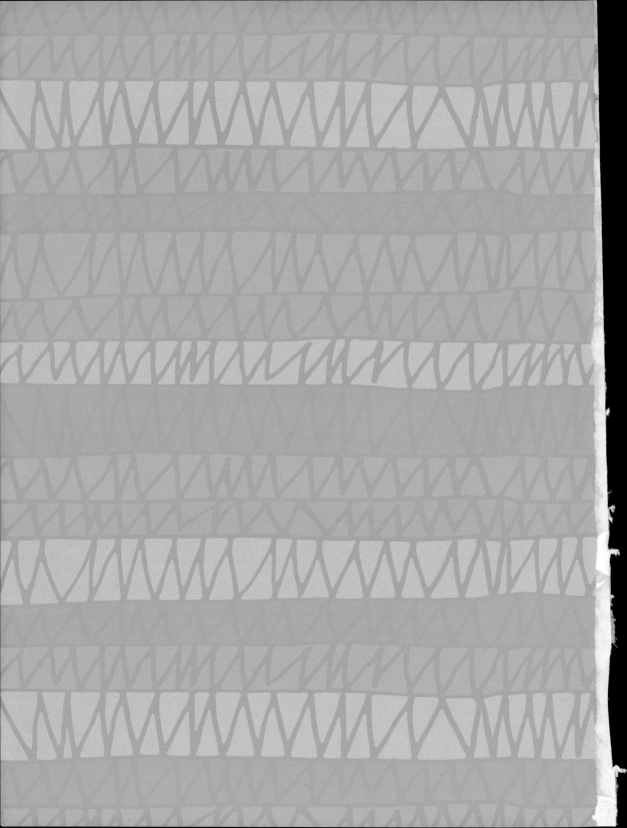

This book belongs to

....

50 Utterly Silly Stories

Compiled by Vic Parker

Miles Kelly

First published in 2012 by Miles Kelly Publishing Ltd
Harding's Barn, Bardfield End Green, Thaxted, Essex, CM6 3PX, UK

Copyright © Miles Kelly Publishing Ltd 2012

This edition printed 2016

10 12 14 15 13 11 9

Publishing Director Belinda Gallagher
Creative Director Jo Cowan
Editorial Director Rosie Neave
Senior Editor Carly Blake
Designers Joe Jones, Simon Lee
Production Elizabeth Collins, Caroline Kelly
Reprographics Stephan Davis, Jennifer Cozens, Thom Allaway
Assets Lorraine King

ISBN 978-1-84810-657-4

Printed in China

British Library Cataloguing-in-Publication Data
A catalogue record for this book is available from the British Library

ACKNOWLEDGEMENTS
The publishers would like to thank the following artists who have contributed to this book:
Cover: Joëlle Dreidemy at The Bright Agency
Beehive Illustration Agency: Rosie Brooks, Mike Phillips
The Bright Agency: Michael Garton
Lisa Bentley, Jan Lewis, Aimee Mappley (decorative frames)
All other artwork from the Miles Kelly Artwork Bank

Made with paper from a sustainable forest

www.mileskelly.net

CONTENTS

Nonsense and Gobbledegook

Tricks and Tomfoolery

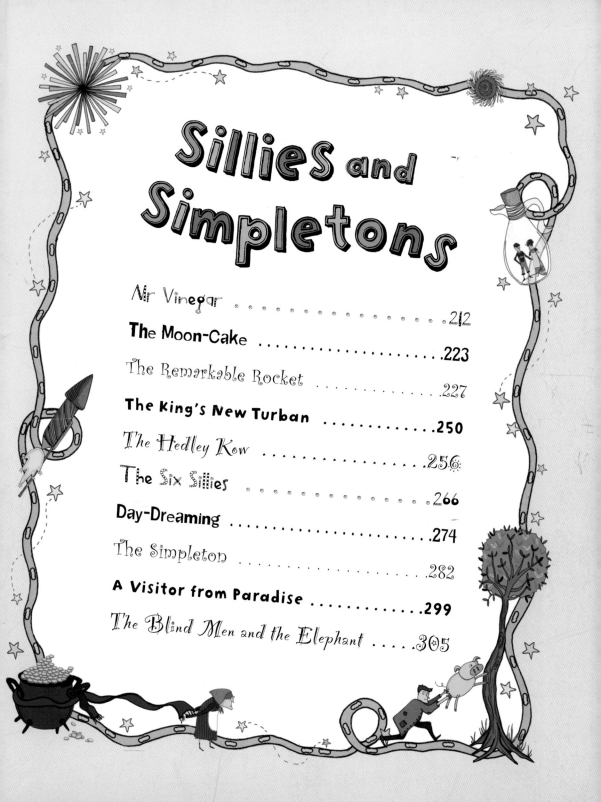

Sillies and Simpletons

Baffled Beasts and Bamboozled Birds

Scarily Stupid, Dangerously Dumb

10

Nonsense
and
Gobbledegook

Down the Rabbit-Hole

An extract from *Alice's Adventures in Wonderland*
by Lewis Carroll

Alice was beginning to get very tired of sitting by her sister on the bank, and of having nothing to do. Once or twice she had peeped into the book her sister was reading, but it had no pictures or conversations in it. 'And what is the use of a book,' thought Alice, 'without pictures or conversation?'

So she was considering (as well as she

could, for the hot day made her feel very
sleepy and stupid) whether the pleasure of
making a daisy-chain would be worth the
trouble of getting up and picking the
daisies, when suddenly a White Rabbit with
pink eyes ran close by her.

There was nothing so *very* remarkable in
that. Nor did Alice think it so *very* much out
of the way to hear the Rabbit say to itself,
"Oh dear! Oh dear! I shall be late!" (When
she thought it over afterwards, it occurred to
her that she ought to have wondered at this,
but at the time it all seemed quite natural.)
When the Rabbit actually *took a watch out of
its waistcoat-pocket*, looked at it, and then
hurried on, Alice started to her feet, for it
flashed across her mind that she had never

seen a rabbit with either a waistcoat-pocket or a watch to take out of it. Burning with curiosity, she ran across the field after it, and fortunately was just in time to see it pop down a large rabbit-hole under the hedge.

In another moment down went Alice after it. The rabbit-hole went straight on like a tunnel for some way, and then dipped suddenly down, so that Alice had not a moment to think about stopping herself before she found herself falling down a well.

First, she tried to look down and make out what she was coming to, but it was too dark to see anything. Then she looked at the sides of the well, and noticed that they were filled with cupboards and bookshelves. Here and there she saw maps and pictures

hung upon pegs. She took down a jar from one of the shelves as she passed. It was labelled ORANGE MARMALADE, but to her great disappointment it was empty. She did not like to drop the jar for fear of killing somebody, so managed to put it into one of the cupboards as she fell past it.

'Well!' thought Alice to herself. 'After such a fall as this, I shall think nothing of tumbling down stairs! How brave they'll all think me at home! Why, I wouldn't say anything about it, even if I fell off the top of the house!' (Which was very likely true.)

Down, down, down. Would the fall *never* come to an end? "I wonder how many miles I've fallen by this time?" she said aloud. "I must be getting somewhere near the centre of the earth. Let me see, that would be four thousand miles down, I think…" (For, you see, Alice had learned several things of this sort in her lessons in the schoolroom, and though this was not a *very* good opportunity for showing off her knowledge, as there was no one to listen to her, still it was good practice to say it over.) "Yes, that's about the right distance – but then I wonder what latitude or longitude I've got to?" (Alice had no idea what latitude was, or longitude either, but thought they were nice grand words to say.)

Presently she began again. "I wonder if I shall fall right *through* the earth! How funny it'll seem to come out among the people that walk with their heads downward! But I

shall have to ask them what the name of the country is, you know. Please, Ma'am, is this New Zealand or Australia?" (And she tried to curtsey as she spoke – fancy *curtseying* as you're falling through the air! Do you think you could manage it?) "And what an ignorant little girl she'll think me for asking! No, it'll never do to ask, but perhaps I shall see it written up somewhere."

Down, down, down. There was nothing else to do, so Alice soon began talking again. "Dinah'll miss me very much tonight, I should think!" (Dinah was the cat.) "I hope they'll remember her saucer of milk at tea-time. Dinah my dear! I wish you were down here with me! There are no

mice in the air, I'm afraid, but you might catch a bat, and that's very like a mouse, you know. But do cats eat bats, I wonder?"

Alice began to get rather sleepy, and went on saying to herself, in a dreamy sort of way, "Do cats eat bats?" and sometimes, "Do bats eat cats?" (For, you see, as she couldn't answer either question, it didn't much matter which way she put it.)

She felt that she was dozing off, and had just begun to dream that she was walking hand in hand with Dinah, and saying to her very earnestly, "Now, Dinah, tell me the truth: did you ever eat a bat?" when suddenly, *thump! thump!* Down she came upon a heap of sticks and dry leaves, and the fall was over.

Alice was not a bit hurt, and she jumped up on to her feet in a moment. She looked up, but it was all dark overhead. Before her was another long passage, and the White Rabbit was still in sight, hurrying down it. There was not a moment to be lost: away went Alice like the wind, and was just in time to hear it say, as it turned a corner, "Oh my ears and whiskers, how late it's getting!"

She was close behind it when she turned the corner, but the

Rabbit was no longer to be seen. She found herself in a long, low hall, which was lit up by a row of lamps hanging from the roof.

There were doors all round the hall, but they were all locked, and when Alice had been all the way down one side and up the other, trying every door, she walked sadly down the middle, wondering how she was ever to get out again…

The Four Little Children Who Went Round the World

By Edward Lear

Once upon a time, a long while ago, there were four little people whose names were Violet, Slingsby, Guy and Lionel, and they all thought they should like to see the world. So they bought a large boat to sail round the world by sea, planning to come back on the other side by land. The boat was painted blue with green spots, and the sail was yellow with red stripes. When they set off, they only took a small Cat to steer and look after the boat, besides an elderly Quangle Wangle, who had to cook the dinner and make the tea, for which they took a large kettle.

For the first ten days they sailed on beautifully, and found plenty to eat as there were lots of fish. They had only to take them out of the sea with a long spoon, when the Quangle Wangle cooked them, and the Pussy Cat was fed with the bones.

During the daytime, Violet chiefly occupied herself in putting salt water into a churn, while her three brothers churned it violently, in the hope that it would turn into butter, which it seldom — if ever — did. In the evening they all settled into the tea kettle, where they all managed to sleep very comfortably, while Pussy and the Quangle Wangle managed the boat.

After a time, they saw some land at a distance, and when they came to it they found it was an island made of water quite surrounded by earth. It was perfectly beautiful, and contained only a single tree, five hundred and three feet high.

When they had landed, they walked about, but found, to their great surprise, that the island was quite full of veal cutlets and chocolate drops, and

24

nothing else. So they all
climbed up the single high tree
to discover, if possible, if there
were any people. Having
remained on the top of the tree
for a week, and not seeing
anybody, they concluded that there
were no inhabitants. When they
came down, they loaded the boat
with two thousand veal cutlets and a
million chocolate drops, and these kept
them going for more than a month as
they voyaged onwards.

After this they came to a shore where
there were no less than sixty-five great
red parrots with blue tails, sitting on a
rail in a row, and all fast asleep.

And I am sorry to say that the Pussy Cat and the Quangle Wangle crept softly, and bit off the tail feathers of all the sixty-five parrots. Violet stuck two hundred and sixty of the feathers in her bonnet, so it looked lovely and glittering.

Next, they came to a narrow part of the sea which was so entirely full of fishes that the boat could go on no farther: so they remained there about six weeks, feasting on them. Many of the uneaten fish complained of the cold, as well as of the difficulty they had in getting any sleep on account of the

extreme noise made by the neighbouring
Arctic bears, so Violet knitted small woollen
frocks for them. Then they were quite warm
and slept soundly.

Next, they came to a country that was
covered with immense orange trees, quite
full of fruit. So they all landed, taking with
them the tea kettle, intending to gather
some of the oranges in it. But a most
dreadfully high wind rose, and the oranges
fell down on their heads by millions and
millions. They thumped and bumped them
all so seriously, that they were obliged to
run as hard as they could for their lives.
Besides, the sound of the oranges rattling on
the tea kettle was terrifying!

They got safely to the boat and, after

sailing on calmly for several more days, they came to another country, where they were pleased and surprised to see countless white Mice with red eyes, all sitting in a great circle, slowly eating custard pudding.

As the four travellers were rather hungry, tired of eating fish and oranges for so long a period, Guy asked the Mice for some of their pudding. But no sooner had he finished talking than the Mice turned round and sneezed at him! At this scroobious sound Guy rushed back to the boat.

By and by the four children came to a vast, wide plain, on which nothing could be discovered at first. As the travellers walked on there appeared in the distance an object, which seemed to be somebody in a large white wig, sitting on an armchair made of sponge cakes and oyster shells. Then the Quangle Wangle (who had previously been round the world) exclaimed softly in a loud voice, "It is the cooperative Cauliflower!"

And it was. They soon found that what they had taken for the wig was the top of the Cauliflower, and that he had no feet, being able to walk on a single stalk – which saved him the expense of buying shoes.

Presently, while the party from the boat was gazing at him, he suddenly arose, and, in a plumdomphious manner, hurried off towards the setting sun – accompanied by two Cucumbers – till he finally disappeared over the brink of the western sky.

Shortly after, the travellers sailed below

some high overhanging rocks, from the top of which a little boy dressed in rose-coloured knickerbockers threw an enormous pumpkin at the boat, which hit it and overturned it! Luckily all the party knew how to swim, and they paddled about till after the moon rose, when they righted the boat and boarded it once again.

Two or three days afterwards, they came to a place where they found nothing at all except some wide and deep pits full of mulberry jam. This was the property of tiny, yellow-nosed Apes who store up the mulberry jam for their food in winter, when they mix it with pale periwinkle soup, and serve it out in china bowls, which grow freely all over that part of the country. Only

one of the yellow-
nosed Apes was on
the spot and he was
fast asleep, yet the
four travellers, the Quangle
Wangle and Pussy were so terrified by
the sound of his snoring they merely took a
small cupful of the jam and returned to
their boat without delay.

What was their horror on seeing the boat in the mouth of an enormous Seeze Pyder, a ferocious creature truly dreadful to behold! In a moment, the beautiful boat was bitten into fifty-five thousand million hundred billion bits. It became quite clear that Violet, Slingsby, Guy and Lionel could no longer carry on their voyage by sea.

The four travellers had to make their way on land. Fortunately, there happened to pass by an elderly Rhinoceros, on which they seized, and, all four mounting on his back – the Quangle Wangle sitting on his horn, and the Pussy Cat swinging at the end of his tail – they set off, having only four small beans and three pounds

of mashed potatoes to last them.

They were, however, able to catch
numbers of the chickens, turkeys and other
birds who continually landed on the head
of the Rhinoceros to gather the seeds of the
rhododendron plants which grew there. A
crowd of Kangaroos and gigantic Cranes
accompanied them, and
they went onward in a
triumphant
procession.

In less than eighteen
weeks they all arrived
safely home, where they
were received by their
admiring relatives
with joy.

How the Cow Jumped Over the Moon

An extract from *The Cat and the Fiddle*
by L Frank Baum

Little Bobby was the only son of a small farmer who lived out of town upon a country road. Bobby's mother looked after the house and his father took care of the farm. Bobby himself, who was not very big, helped them both as much as he was able.

It was lonely upon the farm, especially when his father and mother were both busy at work, but the boy had one way to amuse

himself that served to pass many an hour when he would not otherwise have known what to do. He was very fond of music, and his father one day brought him from the town a small fiddle, or violin, which he soon learned to play upon. I don't suppose he was a very fine musician, but the tunes he played pleased himself, as well as his father and mother, and Bobby's fiddle soon became his constant companion.

One day in the warm summer the farmer and his wife determined to drive to the town to sell their butter and eggs and bring back some groceries in exchange for them. While they were gone Bobby was to be left alone.

"We shall not be back till late in the evening," said his mother, "for the weather is too warm to drive very fast. But I have left you a dish of bread and milk for your supper. Be a good boy and amuse yourself with your fiddle until we return."

Bobby promised to be good and look after the house, and then his father and mother climbed into the wagon and drove away to the town.

The boy was not entirely alone, for there was the big black tabby cat lying upon the floor in the kitchen, and the little yellow dog barking at the wagon as it drove away, and the big moolie cow lowing in the pasture down by the brook. Animals are often very good company, and Bobby did not feel nearly as lonely as he would had there been no living thing about the house.

Besides he had some work to do in the garden, pulling up the weeds that grew thick in the carrot bed. When the last faint sounds of the wheels had died away he went into the garden and began his task.

The little dog went too, for dogs love to be with people and to watch what is going on. He sat down near Bobby and cocked up his ears and wagged his tail, and seemed to take a great interest in the Bobby's task of weeding. Once in a while he would rush away to chase a butterfly or bark at a beetle that crawled through the garden,

but he always came back to the boy and
stayed near his side.

By and by the cat, which found it lonely
in the big, empty kitchen, now that Bobby's
mother was gone, came walking into the
garden also, and lay down upon a path in
the sunshine and lazily watched the boy at
his work. The dog and the cat were good
friends, having lived together so long that

they did not care to fight each other. To be sure, Towser (as the little dog was called) sometimes tried to tease pussy, being himself very mischievous. But when the cat put out her sharp claws and showed her teeth, Towser, like a wise little dog, quickly ran away, and so they managed to get along in a friendly manner.

By the time the carrot bed was all weeded, the sun was sinking behind the edge of the forest and the new moon rising in the east. Now Bobby began to feel hungry and went into the house for his dish of bread and milk.

"I think I'll take my supper down to the brook," he said to himself, "and sit upon the grassy bank while I eat it. And I'll take my fiddle, too, and play upon it to pass the time until Father and Mother come home."

It was a good idea, for down by the brook it was cool and pleasant. Bobby took his fiddle under his arm and carried his dish of bread and milk down to the bank that sloped to the edge of the brook. It was rather a steep bank, but Bobby sat upon the edge, and placing his fiddle beside him, leaned against a tree and began to eat his supper.

The little dog had followed at his heels, and the cat also came slowly walking after him. As Bobby ate, they sat one on either side of him and looked earnestly into his face as if they too were hungry. So he threw some of the bread to Towser, who grabbed it eagerly and swallowed it in the twinkling of an eye. Bobby left some of the milk in the dish for the cat, and she came lazily up and drank it in a dainty, sober fashion, and licked both the dish and spoon until no drop of the milk was left.

Then Bobby picked up his fiddle and tuned it and began to play some of the pretty tunes he knew. And while he played he watched the moon rise higher and higher until it was reflected in the smooth, still water of the brook. Indeed, Bobby could not tell which was the plainest to see, the moon in the sky or the moon in the water.

The little dog lay quietly on one side of him, and the cat softly purred upon the

41

other. Even the moolie cow was attracted
by the music and wandered near until she
was browsing the grass at the edge of
the brook.

　　After a time, when Bobby had played all
the tunes he knew, he laid the fiddle down
beside him, near to where the cat slept, and
then he lay down upon the bank and began
to think.

　　It is very hard to think long upon a
dreamy summer night without falling
asleep. Very soon Bobby's eyes closed and he
forgot all about the dog and the cat and the
cow and the fiddle, and dreamed he was
Jack the Giant Killer and was just about to
slay the biggest giant in the world.

　　While he dreamed, the cat sat up and

yawned and stretched herself, and then began wagging her long tail from side to side and watching the moon that was reflected in the water.

But the fiddle lay just behind her, and as she moved her tail, she drew it between the strings of the fiddle, where it caught fast. Then she gave her tail a jerk and pulled the fiddle against the tree, which made a loud noise. This frightened the cat greatly, and not knowing what was the matter with her tail, she started to run as fast as she could. But still the fiddle clung to her tail, and at every step it bounded along and made such a noise that she screamed with terror.

In her fright she ran straight towards the cow, which, seeing a black streak coming at

Nonsense and Gobbledegook

her and hearing the racket made by the fiddle, also became frightened and made such a jump to get out of the way that she leapt right across the brook, over the very spot where the moon shone in the water!

Bobby had been awakened by the noise, and opened his eyes in time to see the cow jump. At first it seemed to him that she had actually jumped over the moon in the sky, instead of the one in the brook.

The little dog laughed to see such fun caused by the cat, and ran barking and dancing along the bank, so that he knocked against the dish, and behold! It slid down the bank, carrying the spoon with it, and the dish ran away with the spoon into the water of the brook with a splash.

As soon as Bobby recovered from his surprise he ran after the cat, which had raced to the house, and soon came to where the fiddle lay upon the ground, it having at last dropped from the cat's tail. He examined it carefully and was glad to find it was not hurt, in spite of its rough usage. Then he had to go across the brook and drive the cow back over the little bridge, and also to roll up his sleeve and reach into the water to recover the dish and the spoon.

Then he went back to the house and lit a lamp, and sat down to while away the time before his father and mother returned by composing a new tune…

Master of All Masters

By Joseph Jacobs

A girl once went to the fair to offer her services as a servant. At last a funny-looking old gentleman hired her and took her home to his house. There, he told her that he had something to teach her, for that in his house he had his own names for many things.

He said to her: "What will you call me?"

"Master or mister, or whatever you

please sir," says she.

He said: "You must call me 'master of all masters'. And what would you call this?" pointing to his bed.

"Bed or couch, or whatever you please, sir."

"No, that's my 'barnacle'. And what do you call these?" said he pointing to his pantaloons.

"Breeches or trousers, or whatever you please, sir."

"You must call them 'squibs and crackers'. And what would you call her?" pointing to the cat.

"Cat or kit, or whatever you please, sir."

"You must call her 'white-faced simminy'. And this now," showing the fire,

"what would you call this?"

"Fire or flame, or whatever you please, sir."

"You must call it 'hot cockalorum', and what would you call this?" he went on, pointing to the water.

"Water or wet, or whatever you please, sir."

"No, 'pondalorum' is its name. And what do you call all this?" asked he, as he pointed to the house.

"House or cottage, or whatever you please, sir."

"You must call it 'high topper mountain'," said he.

That very night the servant woke her master up in a fright and said:

"Master of all masters, get out of your barnacle and put on your squibs and crackers. For white-faced simminy has got a spark of hot cockalorum on its tail, and unless you get some pondalorum, high topper mountain will be all on hot cockalorum!"

That's all.

The Accomplished and Lucky Teakettle

By A B Mitford

A long time ago at a temple called Morinji, in the province of Jhôsiu, there was an old teakettle. One day, when the temple priest was about to hang it over the hearth to boil water for his tea, the kettle suddenly sprouted the head and tail of a badger.

What a wonderful kettle, to come out all over with fur!

The priest, thunderstruck, called in the youngest monks of the temple to see the sight. Whilst they were stupidly staring, one suggesting one thing and another another thing, the kettle jumped up into the air and began flying about the room. More astonished than ever, the priest and his pupils tried to chase it, but no thief or cat was ever half so sharp as this wonderful badger-kettle.

At last, however, they managed to knock it down and secure it. Holding it in with their joint efforts, they forced it into a

box, intending to carry it off and throw it away in some distant place, so that they might be no more plagued by the goblin.

For this day their troubles were over, but, as luck would have it, the tinker who was in the habit of working for the temple called in. The priest suddenly thought that it was a pity to throw the kettle away for nothing, and he might as well get a small amount for it, no matter how tiny.

So he brought out the kettle, which had gone back to its former shape, and showed it to the tinker. When the tinker saw the kettle, he offered twenty copper coins for it, and the priest was only too glad to close the bargain and be rid of the troublesome piece. The tinker trudged off home with his new purchase.

That night, as the tinker lay asleep, he heard a strange noise near his pillow. He peered out from under the bedclothes, and there he saw the kettle covered with fur and walking about on four legs. The tinker started up in a fright to see what it could all mean, when all of a sudden the kettle went back to its former shape. This happened over and over again, until at last the tinker showed the teakettle to a friend, who said: "This is certainly an accomplished and lucky teakettle. You should take it about as a show, with songs and music, and make it

dance and walk on the tightrope."

The tinker, thinking this good advice, made arrangements with a showman, and set up an exhibition. The noise of the kettle's performances soon spread abroad. Even the Princes of the land sent to order the tinker to come to them, and he grew rich beyond all his expectations. Even the Princesses, too, and the great ladies of the court, took great delight in the dancing kettle, so that no sooner had it shown its tricks in one place than it was time for them to keep some other engagement.

At last the tinker grew so rich that he took the kettle back to the temple, where it was laid up as a precious treasure, and worshipped as a saint.

Boots Who Made the Princess Say, "That's a Story"

By Sir George Webbe Dasent

Once on a time there was a king who had a daughter, and she was such a dreadful storyteller that the like of her was not to be found far or near. So the king sent out word that if anyone could tell such a string of lies that would get her to say, "That's a story," he could have her for his wife, and half the kingdom too. Many came to try their luck, for everyone would have been very glad to have the Princess, to say nothing of the kingdom. But they all cut a sorry figure, for the Princess was so given to storytelling that their lies went in one ear and out the other.

Among the rest came three brothers. The two elder went first, but they fared no better than those who had gone before. Last of all, the third brother, Boots, set off and found the Princess in the farmyard.

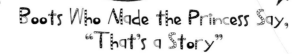
"Good morning," he said, "and thank
you for nothing."

"Good morning," said she, "and the same
to you."

Then she went on, "You haven't such a
fine farmyard as ours, I'll be bound. For
when two shepherds stand, one at each end
of it, and blow their ram's horns, one can't
hear the other."

"Haven't we though!" answered Boots.
"Ours is far bigger. For when a cow begins
to go with calf at one end of it, she doesn't
get to the other end before the time to drop
her calf is come."

"I dare say!" said the Princess. "Well, but
you haven't such a big ox, after all, as ours
yonder. For when two men sit, one on each

horn, they can't touch each other with a ginormous ruler."

"Stuff!" said Boots. "Is that all? Why, we have an ox who is so big, that when two men sit, one on each horn, and each blows his great mountain trumpet, they can't hear one another."

"I dare say," said the Princess. "But you haven't so much milk as we, I'll be bound.

For we milk our cattle into great pails,
and carry them indoors and empty them
into great tubs, and so we make great,
great cheeses."

"Oh! you do, do you?" said Boots. "Well,
we milk ours into great tubs, and then we
put them in carts and drive them indoors,
and then we turn them out into great
brewing vats, and so we make cheeses as

61

big as a great house. We had, too, a pony to tread the cheese well together when it was making, but once she tumbled down into the cheese, and we lost her. After we had eaten at this cheese seven years, we came upon the pony, alive and kicking.

"Well, once after that I was going to drive this pony to the mill, and her backbone snapped in two, but I wasn't put out, not I, for I took a young tree, and put it into her for a backbone, and she had no other backbone all the while we had her. But the sapling grew up into such a tall tree, that I climbed right up to heaven by it, and when I got there, I saw the Virgin Mary sitting and spinning the foam of the sea into pigs'-bristle ropes. But just then the tree

broke short off, and I couldn't get down
again, so the Virgin Mary let me down by
one of the ropes. Down I slipped, straight
into a fox's hole, and who should sit there
but my mother and your father cobbling
shoes. Just as I stepped in, my mother gave
your father such a box on the ear, that it
made his whiskers curl."

"That's a story!" said the Princess. "My
father never did any such thing in all his
born days!"

So Boots got to marry the Princess and
won half the kingdom besides.

A Silly Question

By E Nesbit

"**H**ow do you come to be white, when all your brothers are tabby?" Dolly asked her kitten. As she spoke, she took it away from the ball it was playing with, and held it up and looked in its face as Alice did with the Red Queen.

"I'll tell you if you'll keep it a secret, and not hold me so tight," the kitten answered.

Dolly was not surprised to hear the

kitten speak, for she had read fairy books and she knew that all creatures answer if one only speaks to them properly. So she held the kitten more comfortably and the tale began.

"You must know, my dear Dolly," the kitten began, sounding as though it had always known Dolly very well, "you must know that when we were very small we all set out to seek our fortunes—"

"Why," interrupted Dolly, "you were all born and brought up in our barn! I used to see you every day."

"Quite so," said the kitten, "we sought our fortune every night, and it turned out to be mice, mostly. Well, one night I was seeking mine, when I came to a hole in the door that I had never noticed before. I crept through it and found myself in a beautiful large room. It smelled delicious. There was cheese there, and fish, and cream, and mice, and milk. It was the most lovely room you can think of."

"There's no such room—" began Dolly.

"Well, I stayed there some time," continued the kitten. "It was the happiest hour of my life. But, as I was washing my face after one of the most delicious herring's heads you ever tasted, I noticed that on nails all round the room were hung skins – and they were cat skins," the kitten added slowly. "Well may you tremble!"

Dolly hadn't trembled. She had only shaken the kitten to make it speak faster.

"Well, I stood there rooted to the ground
with horror, and then came a sort of
horrible scramble-rush, and a barking and
squeaking, and a terrible monster stood
before me. It was something like a dog and
something like a broom, something like
being thrown out of the larder by cook – I
can't describe it. It caught me up, and in less

than a moment it had hung my tabby skin on a nail behind the door. I crept out of that lovely fairyland a cat without a skin. And that's how I came to be white."

"I don't quite see—" began Dolly.

"No? Why, what would your mother do if someone took off your dress, and hung it on a nail where she could not get it?"

"Buy me another, I suppose."

"Exactly. But when my mother took me to the cat-skin shop, they were, unfortunately, quite out of tabby dresses in my size, so I had to have a white one."

"I don't believe a word of it," said Dolly.

"No? Well, I'm sure it's as good a story as you could expect in answer to such a silly question."

"But you were always—"

"Oh, well!" said the kitten, showing its claws, "if you know more about it than I do, of course there's no more to be said. Perhaps you could tell me why your hair is brown?"

"I was born so, I believe," said Dolly gently.

The kitten put its nose in the air.

"You've got no imagination," it said.

"But Kitty, really and truly, without pretending, you were born white, you know."

"If you know all about it, why did you ask me? At any rate, you can't expect me to remember whether I was born white or not. I was too young to notice such things."

"Now you are in fun," said poor Dolly, bewildered.

The kitten bristled with indignation.

"What! You really don't believe me? I'll never speak to you again," the kitten said. And it never has.

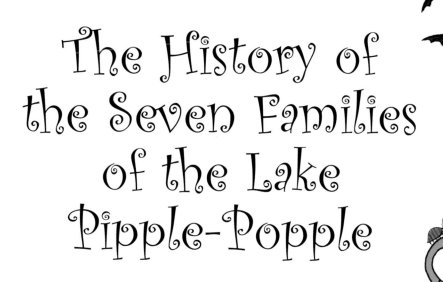

The History of the Seven Families of the Lake Pipple-Popple

By Edward Lear

Introductory

In former days – that is to say, once upon a time – there lived in the Land of Gramble-Blamble seven families. They lived by the side of the great Lake Pipple-Popple (one of the seven families, indeed, lived in the lake), and on the outskirts of the city of Tosh. The names of all these places you

have probably heard of and you have only
not to look in your geography books to
find out about them.

Now, the seven families who lived on the
borders of the great Lake Pipple-Popple
were as follows in the next chapter.

The Seven Families

There was a family of two old Parrots and
seven young Parrots.

There was a family of two old Storks
and seven young Storks.

There was a family of two old
Geese and seven young Geese.

There was a family of
two old Owls and seven
young Owls.

There was a family of two old Guinea
Pigs and seven young Guinea Pigs.

There was a family of two old Cats and
seven young Cats.

And there was a family of two old Fishes
and seven young Fishes.

The Habits of the Seven Families

The Parrots lived upon the beautiful
Soffsky-Poffsky trees, which were covered
with blue leaves, and they fed upon
fruit, artichokes and
striped beetles.

75

The Storks walked in and out of the Lake Pipple-Popple, and ate frogs for breakfast, and buttered toast for tea, but on account of the extreme length of their legs they could not sit down, and so they walked about continually.

The Geese, having webs to their feet, caught quantities of flies, which they ate for dinner.

The Owls anxiously looked after mice, which they caught, and made into sago puddings.

The Guinea Pigs toddled about the gardens, and ate lettuces and Cheshire cheese.

The Cats sat still in the sunshine, and fed upon sponge biscuits.

The Fishes lived in the lake, and fed chiefly on boiled periwinkles.

And all these seven families lived together in the utmost fun and happiness.

The Children of the Seven Families Are Sent Away

One day all the seven fathers and the seven mothers of the seven families agreed to send their children out to see the world.

They called them all together, and gave them each eight shillings and some good advice, some chocolate drops, and a small green Morocco pocket book to write down what they had spent in, and begged them above all *not to quarrel.* Then the children of each family thanked their parents, and, making in all forty-nine polite bows, they went into the wide world.

The History of the Seven Young Parrots

The seven young Parrots had not gone far when they saw a tree with a single cherry on it, which the oldest Parrot picked instantly, but the other six, being extremely hungry, tried to get it also. On which all the seven began to fight, and they scuffled, and huffled, and ruffled, and shuffled, and puffled, and muffled, and buffled, and duffled, and fluffled, and guffled, and bruffled, and screamed, and shrieked, and squealed, and squeaked, and clawed, and snapped, and bit, and bumped, and

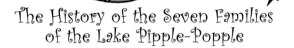

thumped, and dumped, and flumped each other, till they were all torn into little bits. At last there was nothing left to record this painful incident except the cherry and seven small green feathers.

And that was the end of the seven young Parrots.

The History of the Seven Young Storks

When the seven young Storks set out, they walked or flew for fourteen weeks in a straight line, and for six weeks more in a crooked one, and then they ran as hard as they could for one hundred and eight miles. After that they stood still and made a chatter-clatter-blattery noise with their bills.

77

About the same time they saw a large frog, spotted with green, and with a sky-blue stripe under each ear. So, being hungry, they immediately flew at him, and began to quarrel as to which of his legs should be taken off first. One said this and another said that, and while they were all quarrelling, the frog hopped away.

When they saw that he was gone, they began to chatter-clatter, blatter-platter, patter-blatter,

matter-clatter, flatter-quatter, more
violently than ever. After they had fought
for a week, they pecked each other all to
little pieces, so that at last nothing was
left of any of them except their bills.

And that was the end of the seven
young Storks.

The History of the Seven
Young Geese

When the seven young Geese began
to travel, they went over a large
plain, on which there was but one
tree. So four of them went up to the
top of it and looked about them,
while the other three waddled up and
down and repeated poetry.

Presently they saw, a long way off, a curious object with a perfectly round body resembling a boiled plum pudding, with two little wings, and a beak, and three feathers growing out of his head, and only one leg.

So, after a time, all the seven young Geese said to each other, "Beyond all doubt this beast must be a Plum-pudding Flea!"

The Plum-pudding Flea began to hop and skip on his one leg and came straight to the tree, where he stopped and looked about him angrily.

The seven young Geese were greatly alarmed, and all of a tremble-bemble.

The Plum-pudding Flea skipped and hopped about more and more, and higher and higher. Then he opened his mouth and

began to bark so loudly
that they were
unable to bear the
noise and every one
of them suddenly
tumbled down
quite dead.

So that was the end of the
seven young Geese.

The History of the Seven
Young Owls

When the seven young Owls set out, they
sat every now and then on the branches of
old trees, and never went far at one time.
One night, when it was quite dark, they
thought they heard a mouse, but, as the gas

83

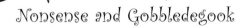
lamps were not lit, they could not see him.

So they called out, "Is that a mouse?"

On which a mouse answered, "Squeaky-peeky-weeky! Yes, it is!"

Immediately all the young Owls threw themselves off the tree, meaning to land on the ground, but they did not see that there was a large well below them, into which they all fell, and every one of them was drowned in less than half a minute.

And that was the end of the seven young Owls.

The History of the Seven Young Guinea Pigs

The seven young Guinea Pigs went into a garden full of gooseberry bushes and tiggory trees, under which they fell asleep. When they awoke, they saw a large lettuce, which had grown out of the ground while they had been sleeping, and which had an immense number of delicious-looking green leaves. Instantly the seven young Guinea Pigs rushed with such extreme force against the lettuce plant, and hit their heads so hard against its stalk, that all seven were killed.

That was the end of the seven young Guinea Pigs.

The History of the Seven Young Cats

The seven young Cats set off on their travels with great delight. But, on coming to the top of a high hill, they perceived at a

Clangle Wangle and ran straight up to it.

Now, the Clangle Wangle is a most dangerous beast, and by no means commonly to be met with. The moment the Clangle Wangle saw the seven young Cats approach, he ran away. As he ran straight on for four months, and the Cats, though they continued to run, could never overtake him, they all gradually died of exhaustion, and never afterwards recovered.

And that was the end of the seven young Cats.

The History of the Seven Young Fishes

The seven young Fishes swam across the Lake Pipple-Popple, and into the river, and into the ocean, where, most unhappily for them, they saw, on the fifteenth day of their travels, a bright-blue Boss-Woss, and instantly swam after him. But the Blue Boss-Woss plunged into soft mud where, in fact, his house was. And the seven young Fishes also plunged into the mud quite against their will, and, not being accustomed to it, were all suffocated in a very short period.

And that was the end of the seven young Fishes.

Of What Occurred Subsequently

After it was known that the seven young Parrots, and the seven young Storks, and the seven young Geese, and the seven young

Owls, and the seven young Guinea Pigs, and the seven young Cats, and the seven young Fishes, were all dead, the Frog, and the Plum-pudding Flea, and the Mouse, and the Clangle Wangle, and the Blue Boss-Woss, all met together to rejoice. They gave a tea party, and a garden party, and a ball, and a concert, and then returned to their respective homes full of joy.

Of What Became of the Parents of the Forty-Nine Children

When the two old Parrots, and the two old Storks, and the two old Geese, and the two old Owls, and the two old Guinea Pigs, and the two old Cats, and the two old Fishes, became aware, by reading in the newspapers, of the tragic death of the whole of their families, they refused all further food. Sending out to various shops, they purchased great quantities of Cayenne pepper and brandy and vinegar and blue sealing wax, besides seven immense glass

The Finest Liar in the World

By Andrew Lang

At the edge of a wood there lived an old man who had only one son. One day he called the boy to him and said he wanted some corn ground, but the youth must be sure never to enter any mill where the miller was beardless.

The boy took the corn and set out.

Before he had gone very far he saw a large mill in front of him, with a beardless man standing in the doorway.

"Good greeting, beardless one!" cried he.

"Good greeting, sonny," replied the man.

"Could I grind something here?"

"Yes, certainly! I will finish what I am doing and then you can grind as long as you like."

But suddenly the boy remembered what his father had told him, and bade farewell to the man. He went further down the river till he came to another mill,

91

not knowing that as soon as his back was turned the beardless man had picked up a bag of corn and run hastily to the same mill before him.

When the boy reached the second mill, and saw a second beardless man sitting there, he did not stop, and walked on till he came to a third mill. But this time also the beardless man had been too clever for him, and had arrived first by another road. When it happened a fourth time the boy grew cross. He said to himself, "It is no good going on. There seems to be a beardless man in every mill," and he took his sack from his back, and made up his mind to grind his corn where he was.

The beardless man finished grinding his

own corn, and when he had done he said to
the boy, who was beginning to grind his,
"Suppose, sonny, we make a cake of what
you have there."

Now the boy had been rather uneasy
when he remembered his father's words,
but he thought to himself, 'What is done
cannot be undone,' and answered, "Very
well, let it be."

Then the beardless one got up, threw the
flour into the tub and made a hole in the
middle, telling the boy to fetch some water
from the river in his two hands to mix the
cake. When the cake was ready for baking
they put it on the fire, and covered it with
hot ashes, till it was cooked through. Then
they leaned it up against the wall, for it was

too big to go into a cupboard, and the beardless one said to the boy: "Look here, sonny, if we share this cake we shall neither of us have enough. Let us see who can tell the biggest lie, and the one who lies the best shall have the whole cake."

The boy, not knowing what else to do, answered, "All right, you begin."

So the beardless one began to lie with all his might, and when he was tired of inventing new lies the boy said to him, "My good fellow, if *that* is all you can do it is not much! Listen to me, and I will tell you a true story.

"In my youth, when I was an old man, we had a quantity of beehives. Every morning when I got up I counted them over, and it was quite easy to number the bees, but I never could reckon the hives properly. One day, as I was counting the bees, I discovered that my best bee was missing, and without losing a moment I saddled a cock and went out to look for him. I traced him as far as the shore, and knew that he had crossed the sea, and that I must follow. When I had reached the other side I found a man had harnessed my bee to a plough, and with his help was sowing millet seed.

"I shouted to him, 'That is my bee! Where did you get him from?'

"The man replied, 'Brother, if he is yours, take him,' and he not only gave me back my bee, but a sack of millet seed into the

bargain, because he had made use of my
bee. Then I put the bag on my shoulders,
took the saddle from the cock and placed it
on the back of the bee, which I mounted,
leading the cock by a string, so that he
should have a rest. As we were flying home
over the sea one of the
strings that held the
bag of millet broke

in two, and the sack dropped straight into the ocean. It was quite lost, of course, and there was no use thinking about it, and by the time we were safe back again night had come. I then got down from my bee, and let him loose so that he might get his supper, gave the cock some hay, and went to sleep myself. But when I awoke with the sun what a scene met my eyes! During the night, wolves had come and had eaten my bee. And honey lay ankle-deep in the valley and knee-deep on the hills. Then I began to consider how I could best collect some to take home with me.

"Now it happened that I had with me a small hatchet, and this I took to the wood, hoping to meet some animal which I could

97

kill, whose skin I might turn into a bag. As I entered the forest I saw two roe deer hopping on one foot, so I slew them with a single blow, and made three bags from their skins, all of which I filled with honey and placed on the back of the cock.

"At length I reached home, where I was told that my father had just been born, and that I must go to fetch some holy water to sprinkle him with. As I went I turned over in my mind if there was no way for me to get back my millet seed, which had dropped into the sea. When I arrived at the place with the holy water I saw the seed had fallen on fruitful soil, and was growing before my eyes. More than that, it was cut by an invisible hand and made into a cake.

"So I took the cake as well as the holy water, and was flying back with them over the sea, when there fell a great rain, and the sea was swollen, and swept away my millet cake. Ah, how vexed I was at its loss when I was safe on earth again.

"Suddenly I remembered that my hair was very long. If I stood it touched the ground, although if I was sitting it only reached my ears. I seized a knife and cut off a large lock, which I plaited together, and, when night came, tied it into a knot and prepared to use it for a pillow. But what was I to do for a fire? A tinder box I had, but no wood. Then it occurred to me that I had stuck a needle in my clothes, so I took the needle and split it in pieces, and lit it, then

laid myself down by the fire and went to
sleep. But while I was sleeping a spark from
the fire lighted on the hair, which was
burned up in a moment. In despair I threw
myself on the ground, and
instantly sank in it as
far as my waist. I
struggled to get
out but only fell
in further, so I ran to
the house, seized a spade, dug myself out,
and took home the holy water.

"On the way I noticed that the ripe
fields were full of reapers, and suddenly the
air became so frightfully hot that the men
dropped down in a faint. Then I called to
them, 'Why don't you bring out our mare,

which is as tall as two days and as broad as half a day, and make a shade for yourselves?' My father heard what I said and jumped quickly on the mare, and the reapers worked with a will in the shadow, while I snatched up a wooden pail to bring them some water to drink.

"When I got to the well it was frozen hard. In order to draw some water I had to take off my head and break the ice with it. As I drew near them, carrying the water, the reapers all cried out, 'What has become of your head?' I put up my hand and discovered that I really had no head, and that I must have left it in the well. I ran back for it, but found that a fox which was passing by had pulled my head out of the water and was tearing at it. I crept up to him, and gave him such a kick that he uttered a loud scream, and let fall a parchment on which was written: THE CAKE IS MINE AND THE BEARDLESS ONE GOES EMPTY-HANDED."

With these words the boy rose, took the cake, and went home, while the beardless one was left to swallow his disappointment.

A Most Curious Country

An extract from *Through the Looking Glass*
by Lewis Carroll

*At home one day, Alice falls through a looking glass
into the strange world beyond, where weirder and weirder
things happen to her…*

For some minutes Alice stood without speaking, looking out in all directions over the country – and a most curious country it was. There were a number of tiny little brooks running straight across it from side to side, and the ground between was divided up into squares by a number of little green

hedges, that reached from brook to brook.

"I declare it's marked out just like a large chessboard!" Alice said at last. "There ought to be some men moving about somewhere – and so there are!" she added in a tone of delight, and her heart began to beat quick with excitement as she went on. "It's a great huge game of chess that's being played – all over the world – if this *is* the world at all, you know. Oh, what fun it is! How I *wish* I was one of them! I wouldn't mind being a Pawn, if only I might join – though of course I should *like* to be a Queen best.'"

She glanced rather shyly at the real Queen as she said this, who smiled pleasantly, and said, "That's easily managed. You can

ears, and almost blowing her hair off her head, she fancied.

"Now! Now!" cried the Queen. "Faster! Faster!" And they went so fast that at last they seemed to skim through the air, hardly touching the ground with their feet, till suddenly, just as Alice was getting quite exhausted, they stopped, and she found herself sitting on the ground, breathless and giddy.

The Queen propped her up against a tree, and said, "You may rest a little now."

Alice looked round her in great surprise. "I do believe we've been under this tree the whole time! Everything's just as it was!"

"Of course it is," said the Queen, "what would you have it?"

"Well, in *our* country," said Alice, still panting a little, "you'd generally get to somewhere else – if you ran very fast for a long time, as we've been doing."

"A slow sort of country!" said the Queen. "Now, *here*, you see, it takes all the running *you* can do, to keep in the same place. If you want to get somewhere else, you must run at least twice as fast as that!"

110

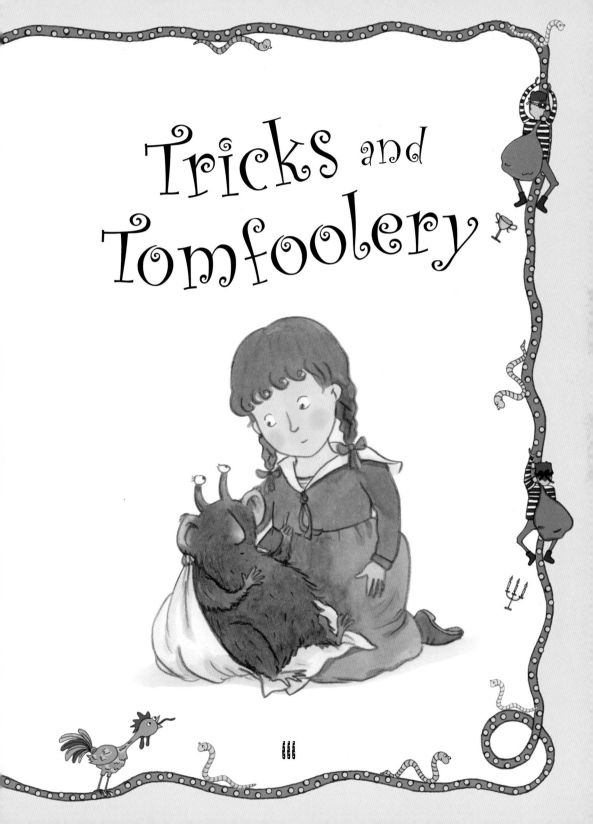

Tricks and Tomfoolery

The Travelling Musicians

By the Brothers Grimm

An honest farmer once had an ass that had been a faithful servant to him for a great many years. But it was now growing old and every day more and more unfit for work. His master therefore was tired of keeping him and began to think of getting rid of him. The ass, who saw that some

mischief was in the wind, took himself slyly off, and began his journey towards the great city. 'For there,' he thought, 'I may become a musician and make my fortune that way.'

After he had travelled a little way, he spied a dog lying by the roadside and panting as if he were tired. "What makes you pant so, my friend?" said the ass.

"Alas," said the dog, "my master was going to knock me on the head because I am old and weak and can no longer make myself useful to him in hunting, so I ran away. What can I do to earn my living?"

"Listen to this," said the ass, "I am going to the great city to become a musician. Suppose you come with me, and try what you can do in the same way?"

The dog said he was willing, and they jogged on together.

They had not gone far before they saw a cat sitting in the middle of the road, looking most downcast. "Hello there, my good lady," said the ass, "what's the matter with you? You look quite out of spirits!"

"Ah, me!" said the cat. "How can one be in good spirits when one's life is in danger? Because I am beginning to grow old, and had rather lie at my ease by the fire than run about the house after mice, my mistress caught me by the scruff of the neck and was going to drown me. Though I have been lucky enough to get away from her, I do not know what is to become of me."

"Oh," said the ass, "by all means come

with us to the great city. You are a good night singer and may make your fortune as a musician."

The cat was pleased with the thought, and joined the party.

Soon afterwards, as they were passing by a farmyard, they saw a cock perched upon a gate, and screaming out with all his might and main.

"Bravo!" said the ass. "Upon my word, you make a famous noise. Pray, what is all this about?"

"Why," said the cock, "I was just now saying that we should have fine weather for our washing day. Yet my mistress and the cook don't thank me for my pains, but threaten to cut off my head tomorrow, and make broth of me for the guests that are coming on Sunday!"

"Heaven forbid!" said the ass. "Come with us, Master Rooster. It will be better, at any rate, than staying here to have your head cut off! Besides, who knows? If we care to sing in tune, we may get up some kind of a concert, so come along with us."

"With all my heart," said the cock, so they all four went on jollily together.

They could not, however, reach the great city the first day. So when night came on, they went into a wood to sleep. The ass and the dog laid themselves down under a great tree, and the cat climbed up into the branches. The cock, thinking that the higher he sat the safer he should be, flew up to the

very top of the
tree and then, as usual,
before he went to sleep, looked out on all
sides of him to see that everything was well.
In doing this, he saw far off something
bright and shining, and calling to his
companions said, "There must be a house
nearby, for I see a light."

"If that be the case," said the ass, "let us
go and see if we can stay there, for our

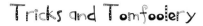

current arrangement is hardly the best in the world!"

"Besides," added the dog, "I should not be the worse for a bone or two, or a nice bit of meat."

So they walked off together towards the spot where the cock had seen the light. As they drew near the light, it became larger and brighter, till they at last came close to a house.

Little did the unfortunate band of animals know that it was a house in which a gang of robbers lived.

The ass, being the tallest of the company, marched up to the window and peeped in. "Well, Donkey," said the cockerel, "what do you see?"

"What do I see?" replied the ass. "Why, I see a table spread with all kinds of good things, and robbers sitting round it making merry."

"That would be a perfect lodging place for us," said the cock.

"Yes," said the ass, "if we could only get in." So they put their heads together and thought hard about how they might be able to get the robbers out, and at last they hit upon a plan.

The ass placed himself upright on his hind legs, with his forefeet resting against the window. The dog got upon his back, the cat scrambled up to the dog's shoulders, and the cock flew up and sat upon the cat's head. When all was ready a signal was

given, and they began their music. The ass
brayed, the dog barked, the cat mewed, and
the cock screamed. Then they all broke
through the window at once, and came
tumbling into the room, amongst the
broken glass, with a most hideous clatter!

The robbers, who had been not a little
frightened by the opening concert, had now
no doubt that some frightful hobgoblin had
broken in upon them, and scampered away
as fast as it could.

Once the coast was clear, our travellers
sat down and gobbled up what the robbers
had left with eagerness. As soon as they had
satisfied themselves, they put out the lights,
and each once more sought out a resting
place to his own liking. The donkey laid

himself down upon a heap of straw
in the yard, the dog stretched himself
upon a mat behind the door, the cat
curled up on the hearth before the warm
ashes, and the cock perched upon a beam
on the top of the house. They were all tired
with their journey, and soon fell asleep.

About midnight, when the robbers saw
from afar that the lights were out and all
seemed quiet, they began to think that they
had been in too great a hurry to run away.
One of them went to see what was going
on. Finding everything still, he marched into
the kitchen and groped about till he found
a match to light a candle. Then, spying the
glittering fiery eyes of the cat, he mistook
them for live coals, and held the match to

them to light it. The cat, not understanding this joke, sprang at his face and scratched at him. This frightened the robber dreadfully, and away he ran to the back door. There the dog jumped up and bit him on the leg, and as he was crossing over the yard the ass kicked him, and the cock, who had been awakened by the noise, crowed with all his might.

At this the robber ran back as fast as he could to his comrades, and told the captain how a horrid witch had

123

got into the house, and had spat at him and scratched his face with her long bony fingers, how a man with a knife in his hand had hidden himself behind the door and stabbed him in the leg, how a black monster stood in the yard and struck him with a club, and how the devil had sat upon the top of the house and cried, "Throw the rascal up here!"

After this the robbers never dared to go back to the house. The musicians were so pleased with their quarters that they took up their abode there, and there they are, I dare say, to this very day.

The Field of Boliauns

By Joseph Jacobs

One fine day at harvest, in holiday time, when the sun blazed high over the cornfields, Tom Fitzpatrick was taking a ramble through the country. He went along the shady side of a field, when all of a sudden he heard a clacking sort of noise a little before him in the hedgerow.

"Dear me," said Tom, "but isn't it surprising to hear the stone-chatters singing so late in the season?" So Tom stole on, going on the tips of his toes to try to get a sight of what was making the noise, to see if he was right in his guess.

The noise stopped, but as Tom looked sharply through the bushes, what should he see in a nook of the hedge but a brown jug, that might hold about a gallon and a half of liquid. By and by a little wee teeny-tiny bit of an old man sauntered up, with a jaunty little hat stuck upon the top of his head. He pulled out a little wooden stool and

stood up upon it, then dipped a little mug into the pitcher, took it out full and put it beside the stool. Then he sat down under the pitcher, and began to work at cobbling a shoe, putting a heel piece on a pointy-toed shoe just fit for himself.

"Well, by the powers," said Tom to himself, "I often heard tell of the Lepracauns, and, to tell God's truth, I never rightly believed in them – but here's one of them in real earnest. If I play my cards right, I can make my fortune. They say a body must never take their eyes off them, or they'll escape."

Tom now stole on a little further, with his eye fixed on the little man just as a cat does with a mouse. When he got up quite close to him, "God bless your work, neighbour," said Tom.

The little man raised up his head, and, "Thank you kindly," said he.

"I wonder why you'd be working on the holiday!" said Tom.

"That's my own business, not yours," was the reply.

"Well, maybe you'd be civil enough to tell us what you've got in the jug there?" said Tom.

"That I will, with pleasure," said he. "It's good beer."

"Beer!" said Tom. "Thunder and fire! Where did you get it?"

"Where did I get it, is it? Why, I made it.

And what do you think I made it of?"

"I haven't a clue," said Tom. "Malt, I suppose, at a guess."

"Wrong!" announced the brownie gleefully. "I made it of heath."

"Of heath!" said Tom, bursting out laughing. "Sure you don't think me to be such a fool as to believe that?"

"Do as you please," said he, "but what I tell you is the truth. Did you never hear tell of the Vikings?"

"Well, what about them?" said Tom.

"Why, when they were here they taught us to make beer out of the heath, and the secret's been in my family ever since."

"Will you give me a taste of your beer?" said Tom.

"I'll tell you what it is, young man, it would be fitter for you to be looking after your father's property than to be bothering decent quiet people with your foolish questions. There now, while you're idling away your time here, the cows have broken into the oats, and are knocking the corn all about."

Tom was taken so by surprise with this that he was just on the very point of turning round… but he suddenly realized that the Lepracaun might be up to a trick. He collected himself, made a grab at the Lepracaun, and caught him up in his hand. However, in his hurry he knocked over the jug and spilled all the beer, so that he could not get a taste of it to tell what sort it was.

Tom then swore that he would kill the Lepracaun if he did not show him where his money was.

Tom looked so wicked and determined that the little man was quite frightened, so said the Lepracaun, "Come along with me a couple of fields off and I will show you a crock of gold."

So they went, and Tom held the Lepracaun fast in his hand, and never took his eyes off him. They had to cross hedges and ditches, and a crooked bit of bog, till at last they came to a great field all full of boliaun plants. The Lepracaun pointed to a big boliaun, and says he, "Dig under that boliaun, and you'll get the great crock all full of guineas."

Tom, in his hurry, had never thought of bringing a spade with him, so he made up his mind to run home and fetch one. So that he might find the right spot when he returned, he took off the red garter on his arm and tied it round the boliaun plant.

Then Tom said to the Lepracaun, "Swear that you won't take that garter away from that boliaun." And the Lepracaun swore right away not to touch it.

"I suppose," said the Lepracaun, very civilly, "you have no further need of me?"

"No," says Tom, "you may go away now, if you please, and God speed you, and may good luck attend you wherever you go."

"Well, goodbye to you, Tom Fitzpatrick," said the Lepracaun, "and much good may it do you when you get it."

So Tom ran for dear life, till he came home and got a spade, and then away with him, as hard as he could go, back to the field of boliauns. But when he got there, lo and behold! Every single boliaun in the field had a red garter tied about it!

"Whatever do I do now?" gasped Tom in exasperation. "I can't dig up the whole field, that's for sure – there's more than forty good Irish acres in it!"

So Tom came home again with his spade on his shoulder, a little cooler than he went, and many's the hearty curse he gave the Lepracaun every time he thought of the turn he had served him.

How the Dragon was Tricked

By Andrew Lang

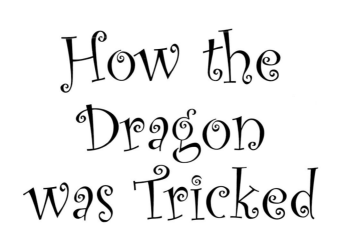

Once upon a time there lived a man who had two sons, but the elder son hated the younger son. One day, as they were walking through a wood, the elder youth seized hold of the other, tied him to a tree, and went on his way hoping that his brother might starve to death.

However, it happened that an old and humpbacked shepherd passed by and said,

"Tell me, my son, why are you tied to that tree?"

"Because I was so crooked," answered the young man, "but it has quite cured me, and now my back is as straight as can be."

"I wish you would bind me to a tree," exclaimed the shepherd, "so that my back would get straight."

"With pleasure," replied the youth. "If you will loosen these cords I will tie you up as firmly as I can."

This was soon done, and then the young man drove off with the shepherd's sheep.

By these and many other tricks the young man soon became so famous that the King demanded to see him. Soldiers captured him and brought him before the

King, who said, "Because of your tricks and pranks, you should, in the eye of the law, be put to death. But if you can bring me the flying horse that belongs to the great dragon, I will spare you."

When night came the young man made his way straight to the dragon's home and the flying horse's stable. He was stretching his hand cautiously out to seize the bridle, when the horse suddenly began to neigh as loud as he could. This woke the sleeping dragon, who was very angry to be disturbed and came to give the horse a beating. The horse was very upset, and when the dragon returned back to bed, he let the young man lead him quietly away.

The King said, "The flying horse is all

very well, but I want something more. You must bring me the covering with the little bells that lies on the bed of the dragon, or I will have you put to death."

When night came the young man went away to the dragon's house and climbed up onto the roof. Then he opened a little window in the roof and let down a rope and tried to hook the bed covering to draw it up. But the little bells began to ring, and the dragon woke and drew the covering towards him, pulling the young man into the room as he did so. Then the dragon flung himself on the youth and bound him fast. He roared to his wife, saying, "Tomorrow when I go out you must stay at home and kill him and cook him. When I

get back we will eat him together."

So the following morning the dragoness took hold of the young man, and reached up on the shelf for a sharp knife with which to kill him. But as she untied the cords the better to get hold of him, the prisoner seized her and threw her into the oven. Then he snatched up the bed covering and carried it to the King.

"That is not enough," said His Majesty. "Bring me the dragon himself, or I will have you put to death."

"It shall be done," answered the youth, and he disguised himself as a beggar and set

out on the road to the dragon's house. The
young man found his enemy in front of his
house, very busy making a box. "What is
the box for?" inquired the beggar.

"It is for the man who killed my wife,
and stole my flying horse and my bed
covering," said the dragon.

"He deserves nothing better," answered
the beggar. "Still that box doesn't look big
enough for a man."

"You are wrong," said the dragon. "The
box is large enough even for me."

"Well, of course, if you can get in, he
should be able to," the man said. "But I am
sure you would find it a tight fit."

"No, there is plenty of room," said the
dragon, tucking himself carefully inside.

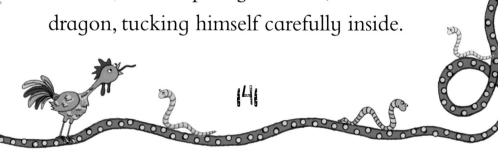

But no sooner was he well in, than the young man clapped the lid on tight, and drove in nails to make it tighter still. Then he took the box on his back and brought it to the King. When the King heard that the dragon was inside, he was so excited that he would not wait. He broke the lock and lifted the lid just a little way. The King was very careful not to leave enough space for the dragon to jump out, but unluckily there was just room for his great mouth.

With one snap the very foolish king vanished down his wide jaws. The young man married the King's daughter and ruled over the land, but what he did with the dragon nobody knows.

The Lad and the Devil

By Sir George Webbe Dasent

Once upon a time there was a lad who was walking along a road cracking nuts. He found one that was worm-eaten, and just at that very moment he met the Devil.

"Is it true, now," said the lad, "what they say, that the Devil can make himself as small as he chooses, and thrust himself in through a pinhole?"

"Yes, it is," said the Devil.

"Oh! It is, is it? Then let me see you do it, and just creep into this nut," said the lad.

So the Devil did it.

Now, when he had crept well into the nut through the worm's hole, the lad stopped it up with a pin. "Now, I've got you safe," he said, and put the nut in his pocket.

When he had walked on a bit, he came to a smithy. He turned in and asked the smith if he'd be good enough to crack that nut for him.

"Ay, that'll be an easy job," said the smith. He took his smallest hammer, laid the nut on the anvil and gave it a blow, but it wouldn't break.

So he took another hammer a little bigger, but that wasn't heavy enough either.

Then he took one bigger still, but it was still the same story, and so the smith got angry, and grasped his great sledgehammer.

"Now, I'll crack you to bits," he said, and let drive at the nut with all his might and main. And so the nut flew to pieces with a bang that blew off half the roof of the smithy, and the whole house creaked and groaned as though it were ready to fall.

"Why! The very Devil himself must have been in that nut," said the smith.

"So he was, you're quite right," said the lad, as he went away laughing.

The Endless Tale

By James Baldwin

Once upon a time in the Far East there was a great king who had no work to do. Every day and day long, he sat on cushions and listened to stories. No matter what the story was about, he never grew tired of hearing it, no matter how long it was.

"There is only one fault that I find with your story," he often said to the storyteller, "it is too short."

Eventually the King hit upon an idea. He sent out a proclamation saying that all the greatest storytellers in the world were invited to his palace. From far and wide they arrived, and some of them told tales that were very long indeed. But the King was always sad when a story came to an end.

At last he sent word into every city and town and country place, offering a prize to anyone who should tell him a tale that had no end at all – a tale that he could enjoy always. He said, "To the man that will tell me a story which shall last forever, I will give my fairest daughter for his wife, and I will make him my heir and he shall be king after me."

But this was not all. He added a very hard condition. "If any man shall try to tell such a story and then fail, he shall have his head cut off."

The King's daughter was very pretty, and there were many young men in that country who were willing to do anything to win her. But none of them wanted to lose their heads, so only a few tried for the prize.

One brave young man invented a story that lasted three months, but at the end of that time he could think of nothing more. His fate was a warning to others, and it was a long time before another storyteller was so rash as to try the King's patience.

But one day a stranger from the South came into the palace. "Great King," he said,

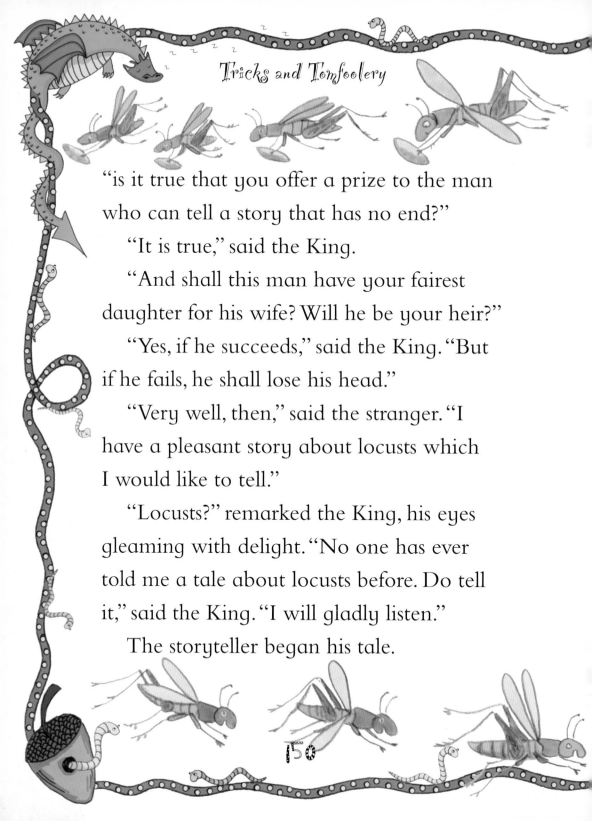

"is it true that you offer a prize to the man who can tell a story that has no end?"

"It is true," said the King.

"And shall this man have your fairest daughter for his wife? Will he be your heir?"

"Yes, if he succeeds," said the King. "But if he fails, he shall lose his head."

"Very well, then," said the stranger. "I have a pleasant story about locusts which I would like to tell."

"Locusts?" remarked the King, his eyes gleaming with delight. "No one has ever told me a tale about locusts before. Do tell it," said the King. "I will gladly listen."

The storyteller began his tale.

"Once upon a time a king seized all the corn in his country, and stored it away in a strong granary. But a swarm of hungry locusts came over the land and saw where the grain had been put. After searching for many days they found on the east side of the granary a teeny-tiny crack that was just large enough for one locust to pass through at a time. So one locust went in and carried away a grain of corn, then another locust went in and carried away a grain of corn, then another locust went in and carried away a grain of corn..."

Day after day, week after week, the man kept on saying, "Then another locust went in and carried away a grain of corn…"

A month passed, a year passed, and still the man kept on saying, "Then another locust went in and carried away a grain of corn…"

At the end of two years, the King said, "How much longer will the locusts be going in and carrying away corn?"

"O King," said the storyteller, "they have as yet cleared only one cubit, and there are many thousand cubits in the granary."

"Man, man," cried the King, "you will drive me mad! I can listen to it no longer. Take my daughter, be my heir, rule my kingdom. But do not let me hear another word about those horrible locusts!"

And so it was that the strange storyteller married the King's daughter, and he lived happily in the land for many years. But his father-in-law, the King, did not care to listen to any more stories.

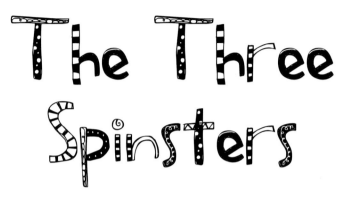

The Three Spinsters

By the Brothers Grimm

There was once a girl who was lazy and would not spin. No matter how her mother tried to persuade her to do it, she simply refused, point blank. At last the mother became angry and lost her patience, and gave the girl a beating so that she cried out loudly. At that moment the Queen was going by. As she heard the crying, she stopped. Going into the house, she asked the mother why she was beating her daughter so that everyone outside in the street could hear her cries.

The woman was ashamed to tell of her daughter's laziness, so she said, "I cannot stop her from spinning. She is forever at it, and I am poor and cannot furnish her with enough flax."

The Queen was delighted and answered, "I like nothing better than the sound of the spinning-wheel, and always feel happy when I hear its humming. Let me take your daughter with me to the castle – I have plenty of flax. She shall spin there to her heart's content."

The mother was only too glad of the

chance to get rid of her lazy, unhelpful
daughter, and the Queen took the girl
with her.

When they reached the castle, the Queen
showed the girl three rooms that were filled
with the finest flax, as full as they could
hold. "Now you can spin me this flax," said
the Queen, "and when you can show it to
me all done you shall have my eldest son
for your bridegroom. You may be poor, but
I make nothing of that – if you prove
yourself to be as hardworking as your
mother led me to believe, that will be good
enough for me."

The girl was inwardly terrified, for she
could not have spun the flax even if she
were to live to be a hundred years old, and

The Three Spinsters

were to sit spinning every day of her life from morning to evening. When she found herself alone she began to weep, and sat so for three days without putting her hand to the spinning-wheel.

On the third day the Queen came, and when she saw that nothing had been done of the spinning she was much surprised. The girl excused herself by saying that she had not been able to begin because of the distress she was in at leaving her home and her mother. The excuse contented the Queen, who said, as she went away, "Tomorrow you must begin to work."

When the girl found herself alone again she could not tell how to help herself or what to do, and in her upset she went and gazed out of the window. There she saw three women passing by. The first of them had a broad flat foot, the second had a big under-lip that hung down over her chin, and the third had a remarkably broad thumb. They all of them stopped in front of the window, and called out to know what it was that the girl wanted. She told them about the awful situation she found herself in. The girl couldn't believe her ears when the three ugly women promised her their help, and said, "Then will you invite us to your wedding, and not be ashamed of us, and call us your cousins, and let us sit at your table? If you will promise this, we will finish off your flax-spinning in a very short time."

"With all my heart," answered the girl, "only come in now, and begin at once." Of course, she would have promised them anything at all to have the spinning done in time to show the Queen!

Then these same women came in, and she cleared a space in the first room for

them to sit and begin their spinning. The
first one drew out the thread and moved the
treddle that turned the wheel. The second
moistened the thread. The third twisted it
and rapped with her finger on the table,
and as often as she rapped, a heap of yarn
fell to the ground, and it was most
beautifully spun.

The girl hid the three spinsters out of the
Queen's sight, and only showed her, as often
as she came, the heaps of well-spun yarn.
There was no end to the praises she
received. When the first room was empty
the women went on to the second, and then
to the third, so that at last all of the flax had
been spun.

Then the three women took their leave,

saying to the girl, "Do not forget what you have promised and it will be all the better for you."

So when the girl took the Queen and showed her the empty rooms and the great heaps of yarn, the wedding was at once arranged. The bridegroom rejoiced that he should have so clever and hardworking a wife, and praised her exceedingly.

"I have three cousins," said the girl, "and as they have shown me a great deal of kindness, I would not wish to forget them in my good fortune. May I be allowed to invite them to the wedding, and to ask them to sit at the table with us?"

The Queen and the bridegroom said at once, "Of course."

So when the feast began, in came the three spinsters in strange guise, and the bride said, "Dear cousins, you are welcome."

"Oh," said the bridegroom, "how did you come to have such dreadfully ugly relations?" Then he went up to the first spinster and said, "How is it that you have such a broad flat foot?"

"With treading," answered she, "with treading."

Then he went up to the second and said, "How is it that you have such a great hanging lip?"

"With licking," answered she, "with licking."

Then he asked the third, "How is it that you have such a broad thumb?"

"With twisting thread," answered she,

163

"with twisting thread."

Then the bridegroom said that from that time forward his beautiful bride should never touch a spinning-wheel.

And so she escaped that tiresome flax-spinning once and for all.

The Stone Soup

A folk tale

Many years ago three soldiers were on their way home from war, hungry and weary of battle, when they came upon a small village. The villagers had suffered a poor harvest because so many of them had been called away to fight. They quickly hid what little food they had and met the three strangers in the village square, moaning about how starving they all were.

The first
soldier said to the villagers,
"Your tired fields have left you nothing
to share. We will share what little we have –
the secret of how to make soup from stones."

A murmur of excitement rippled through
the crowd. Soon a fire was put to the town's
greatest pot. Everyone watched with
curiosity as the soldiers dropped in three
stones. "Now this will be a fine soup," said

the second soldier, "but a pinch of salt and some parsley would make it wonderful!" Up jumped a villager, crying, "I've just remembered where some is!"

She returned with an apronful of parsley and a turnip to boot.

The memory of the villagers strangely seemed to improve. Soon barley, carrots, beef and cream had found their way into the great pot, and even a cask of wine was rolled into the square.

It didn't seem long before everyone was sitting down to a delicious-smelling, rich soup, packed with tasty, chunky vegetables.

The villagers ate and danced and sang well into the night, refreshed by the feast and their new-found friends. They couldn't remember when they had last had such an enjoyable meal. It was the early hours of the morning before everyone finally turned in to bed.

When the three soldiers awoke they found the entire village standing before them. At their feet lay a satchel of the village's best breads and cheese. "You have given us the greatest of gifts – the secret of how to make soup from stones," said an elder, "and we shall never forget."

The third soldier turned to the crowd, and said, "There is no secret, but this is certain – it is only by sharing that we may make a feast."

And off the soldiers wandered down the road, leaving the villagers bewildered but thoughtful behind them.

All Change

By Joseph Jacobs

There was once a man who was the laziest man in all the world. He wouldn't take off his clothes when he went to bed because he didn't want to have to put them on again. He wouldn't raise his cup to his lips, but left it on the table, bent his mouth down to it, and sucked up his tea without lifting the cup up at all. He wouldn't play any sports because he said they made him sweat, and he wouldn't work with his hands for the same reason.

At last he found that he couldn't get anything to eat unless he did some work for it. So he hired himself out to a farmer for the season. But all through the harvest he ate as much and worked as little as he could. When he went to get his wages from his master, all he got was a single pea.

"What do you mean by giving me this?" he said to his master.

"Why, that is all that your labour is worth," was the reply. "You have eaten as much as you have earned."

"None of your cheek," said the man. "Give me my pea, at any rate I have earned that."

So when he got it he went to an inn by
the roadside and said to the landlady, "Can
you give me lodging for the night, me and
my pea?"

"Well, no," said the landlady, "I haven't
got a bed free, but I can take care of your
pea for you."

No sooner said than done. The
pea was lodged with the landlady,
and the laziest man went and
slept in a barn nearby.

The landlady put the pea
upon a dresser and left it there.
A chicken wandering by saw it,
and jumped up
on the dresser
and ate it.

So when the laziest man called the next day and asked for his pea the landlady couldn't find it. She said, "The chicken must have swallowed it."

"Well, I want my pea," said the man. "You had better give me the chicken."

"Why… what… when… how?" stammered the landlady. "The chicken is worth thousands of your pea."

"I don't care for that," sulked the laziest man. "It has got my pea inside it, and the only way I can get my pea is to have that which holds the pea."

"What, give you my chicken for a single pea? Nonsense!" the landlady huffed. "Well, if you

don't I'll summon you before the justice,"
the man threatened.

Then the landlady blustered and flustered
and stamped her foot. "Ah, well," she cried,
"take the chicken and my bad wishes
with it!"

So off went the man very pleased, with
the chicken under his arm and his pea
inside it. He sauntered along all day, till that
night he came to another inn, and asked
the landlord if he and his chicken could
stop there.

The landlord said, "No, no, we have no
room for you, but we can put your chicken
in the stable if you like." So the man said,
"Yes," and went off for the night.

But there was a savage sow in the stable,

and during the night that sow ate up the poor chicken.

When the man came the next morning he said to the landlord, "Please give me my chicken."

"I am awfully sorry, sir," said he, "but my sow has eaten it up."

The laziest man said, "Then give me your sow."

"What, a sow for your chicken? Nonsense. Go away, my man," declared the indignant landlord.

"Well, if you don't do that I'll have you before the justice," declared the laziest man, haughtily.

"Ah, well, take the sow and my curses with it," said the landlord, very angry.

So the laziest man took the sow, with
the chicken inside it and the pea inside the
chicken, and followed along the road till
he came to another inn. He said to the
landlady, "Have you room for me and
my sow?"

"I have not got room for you," said the
landlady, "but I can put your sow up."

So the sow was put in the stable, and the
man went off to lie in the barn for the

night. Now the sow went roaming about the stable, and coming too near the hoofs of a mare, was hit in the forehead and killed.

So when the man came in the morning and asked for his sow the landlady said, "I'm very sorry, sir, but an accident has occurred. My mare has hit your sow in the skull and she is dead."

"What, the mare?" quizzed the baffled man.

"No, your sow," explained the landlady, shamefaced.

The man couldn't believe what he was hearing. "Then give me the mare," he declared.

"What, my mare for your sow? Nonsense!" she scoffed.

"Well, if you don't I'll take you before the justice, then you'll see if it's nonsense," insisted the laziest man.

So after some time the landlady agreed to give the man her mare in exchange for the dead sow.

Then the man followed on in the steps of the mare till he came to another inn, and asked the landlord if he could put him and his mare up for the night. The landlord said, "All our beds are full, but you can put the mare up in the stable if you will."

"Very well," said the man, and he tied the halter of the mare through the ring of the stable.

Early next morning the landlord's daughter said to her father, "That poor mare has had nothing to drink. I'll go and lead it to the river."

"That is none of your business," said the landlord. "Let the man do it himself."

"Ah, but the poor thing has had nothing to drink," said the kind girl. "I'll bring it back very soon." So the girl took the mare to the river bank and let it drink the water, but by chance, the mare slipped into the stream, which was so strong that it carried her away.

The young girl ran back to her father and said, "Oh father, the mare fell into the stream and it was carried quite away. What shall we do? What shall we do?"

When the man came round that morning he said, "Please give me my mare."

"I'm very sorry indeed, sir," explained the landlord, wringing his hands, "My daughter – that one there – wanted to give the poor thing a drink, and took it down to the river, but it fell in and was carried away by the stream. I'm very sorry indeed."

"Your sorrow won't pay my loss," said the man, "the least you can do is to give me your daughter."

"What, my daughter to you because of the mare!" gasped the landlord.

"Well, if you don't I will take you before the justice," stated the laziest man.

Now the landlord didn't like the idea of going before the justice. So after much

haggling he agreed to let his daughter go
with the man. They went along, and they
went along, and they went along, till at last
they came to another inn, which was kept
by the girl's aunt, though the man didn't
know it. So he went in and said, "Can you
give me beds for me and my girl here?"

The landlady looked at the girl, who
said nothing, and replied, "Well, I haven't
got a bed for you but I have got a bed for
her, but perhaps she'll run away."

"Oh, I will manage that," said the man.
He went and got a sack and put the girl in
it and tied her up, and then he went off.

As soon as he was gone the girl's aunt
opened the bag and said, "What has
happened, my dear?" The told her aunt the

whole story. So the aunt took a big dog and put it in the sack. When the man came the next morning, he said, "Where's my girl?"

"There she is," said Auntie, pointing at the sack, "so far as I know."

So the laziest man took the sack and put it on his shoulder, and went along on his way for a time.

Then, as the sun grew high, he sat down under the shade of a tree and thought he would speak to the girl. But when he opened the sack the big dog

flew right out at
him… and that's the
last I heard of him.

Wishing for Wings

An extract from *Five Children and It*
by E Nesbit

*Five children – Cyril, Anthea, Robert, Jane and the youngest, a
baby whom they call 'the Lamb' – move house from London to the
countryside in Kent. In a gravel pit behind their home, they discover
a strange creature called a Psammead, or Sand-fairy. He is able to
grant one wish per day, and, over the next three days, he grants the
children their wishes to become beautiful, to have heaps of gold coins
and for the Psammead to be wanted by everyone. Each foolish wish
causes the children to run into trouble. Fortunately, every day the
Psammead's magic lasts only till sunset…*

Have you ever been up at five o'clock on
a fine summer morning? It is very beautiful.
The sunlight is pinky and yellowy, and all

the grass and trees are covered with dew–
diamonds. All the shadows go the opposite
way to the way they do in the evening,
which is very interesting and makes you feel
as though you were in a new other world.

Anthea awoke at five. She had made
herself wake, and I must tell you how it is
done, even if it keeps you waiting for the
story to go on.

You get into bed at night, and lie down
quite flat on your little back with your
hands straight down by your sides. Then
you say "I must wake up at five" (or six, or
seven, or eight, or nine, or whatever the time
is that you want), and as you say it you
push your chin down on to your chest and
then bang your head back on the pillow.

And you do this as many times as there are ones in the time you want to wake up at. (It is quite an easy sum.) Of course everything depends on your really wanting to get up at five (or six, or seven, or eight, or nine). If you don't really want to, it's all of no use. But if you do – well, try it and see. Of course in this, as in doing Latin prose or getting into mischief, practice makes perfect. Anthea was quite perfect.

At the very moment when she opened her eyes, Anthea heard the black-and-gold clock down in the dining room strike eleven. So she knew it was three minutes to five. The black-and-gold clock always struck wrong, but it was all right when you knew what it meant. It was like a person

talking a foreign language. If you know the
language it is just as easy to understand as
English. And Anthea knew the clock
language.

She was very sleepy, but she jumped out
of bed and put her face and hands into a
basin of cold water. This
is a fairy charm
that prevents your
wanting to get
back into bed
again. Then she
dressed, and
folded up her
nightgown. She
did not tumble
it together by

187

the sleeves, but instead folded it by the seams from the hem, and that will show you the kind of well brought-up little girl she was.

Then Anthea took her shoes in her hand and crept softly down the stairs. She opened the dining room window and climbed out. It would have been just as easy to go out by the door, but the window was more romantic, and less likely to be noticed by Martha, the nanny.

"I will always get up at five," Anthea said to herself. "It is quite too awfully pretty for anything."

Her heart was beating very fast, for she was carrying out a plan quite her own. She could not be sure that it was a good plan, but she was quite sure that it would not be any better if she were to tell the others about it. And she had a feeling that, right or wrong, she would rather go through with it alone.

Anthea put on her shoes under the iron veranda, on the red and yellow shining tiles. Then she ran straight to the sandpit. She quickly found the Psammead's place and dug it out.

It was very cross indeed.

"It's too bad," it said, fluffing up its fur like pigeons do their feathers at Christmas time. "The weather's arctic, and it's the middle of the night."

"I'm so sorry," said Anthea gently. She took off her white pinafore and covered the

Sand-fairy up with it, all but its head, its bat's ears, and its eyes that were like a snail's eyes.

"Thank you," it said, "that's better. What's the wish this morning?"

"I don't know," said she, "that's just it. You see, we've been very unlucky so far. I wanted to talk to you about it. But – would you mind not giving me any wishes till after breakfast? It's so hard to talk to anyone if they jump out at you with wishes you don't really want!"

"You shouldn't say you wish for things if you don't wish for them."

"I'll try not to," said Anthea, "but I do wish—"

"Look out!" said the Psammead in a

warning voice, and it began to blow itself out.

"Oh, this isn't a magic wish — it's just — I should be so glad if you'd not swell yourself out and nearly burst to give me anything just now. Wait till the others are here."

"Well, well," it said indulgently, but it shivered.

"Would you like to come and sit on my lap?" asked Anthea kindly. "You'd be warmer, and I could turn the skirt of my frock up round you. I'd be very careful."

Anthea had never expected that it would, but it did.

"Thank you," it said, "you really are rather thoughtful." It crept on to her lap and snuggled down, and she put her arms

round it with a rather
frightened gentleness.

"Well then," said Anthea,
"everything we have
wished has turned out
rather horrid. I wish
you would advise us.
You are so old, you
must be very wise."

"I was always
generous from a
child," said the
Sand-fairy. "I've spent the whole of my
waking hours giving. But one thing I won't
give – that's advice."

"You see," Anthea went on, "it's such a
wonderful thing – such a splendid, glorious

chance. It's so good and kind and dear of
you to give us our wishes, and it seems such
a pity it should all be wasted just because
we are too silly to know what to wish for."

Anthea had meant to say that – and she
had not wanted to say it before the others.
It's one thing to say you're silly, and quite
another to say that other people are.

"Child," said the Sand-fairy sleepily,
"I can only advise you to think before
you speak…"

"But I thought you never gave advice."

"That piece doesn't count," it said.
"You'll never take it! Besides, it's not
original. It's in all the copy books."

"But won't you just say if you think
wings would be a silly wish?"

"Wings?" it said. "I should think you might do worse. Only, take care you aren't flying high at sunset. There was a little Ninevite boy I heard of once. He was one of King Sennacherib's sons, and a traveller brought him a Psammead. He used to keep it in a box of sand on the palace terrace. It was a dreadful degradation for one of us, of course. Still, the boy was the Assyrian King's son.

"One day," continued the Sand-fairy, "he wished for wings and got them. But at sunset, the wings turned into stone, and he fell slap onto one of the winged lions at the top of his father's great staircase, and what with *his* stone wings and the lion's stone wings – well, it's not a pretty story! But I believe the boy enjoyed himself very much till then… Goodbye. I *am* so sleepy."

It jumped off her lap, dug frantically, and vanished.

Anthea was late for breakfast. Afterwards, she and the others went back to the sand-pit, without the Lamb. In the lane Anthea, breathless from scurrying about, panted out, "I want to propose we take turns to wish. Only, nobody's to have a wish if the others don't think it's a nice wish. Do you agree?"

"Who's to have first wish?" asked Robert cautiously.

"Me, if you don't mind," said Anthea apologetically. "And I've thought about it – and it's wings."

There was a silence. The others rather wanted to find fault, but it was hard because the word 'wings' raised a flutter of joyous excitement in every breast.

"Not so dusty," said Cyril generously, and Robert added, "Really, Panther, you're not quite such a fool as you look."

Jane said, "I think it would be perfectly lovely. It's like a bright, joyful dream."

They found the Sand-fairy easily.

Anthea said, "I wish we all had beautiful wings to fly with."

The Sand-fairy blew himself out, and next moment each child felt a funny feeling, half heaviness and half lightness, on its shoulders.

Then the Psammead put its head on one

side and turned its snail's eyes from one child to the other. "Not so dusty," it said dreamily. "But really, Robert, you're not quite such an angel as you look." Robert almost blushed.

The wings were very big, and more beautiful than you can possibly imagine – for they were soft and smooth, and every feather lay neatly in its place. And the feathers were of the most lovely mixed changing colours, like the rainbow, or iridescent glass, or the beautiful scum that sometimes floats on water that is not at all nice to drink.

"Oh – but can we fly?" Jane said, standing anxiously, first on one foot and then on the other.

"Look out!" said Cyril. "You're treading on my wing."

"Does it hurt?" asked Anthea with interest, but no one answered, for Robert had spread his wings and jumped up, and now he was slowly rising in the air. He looked very awkward in his knickerbocker suit – his boots in particular hung helplessly, and seemed much larger than when he was standing in them. But the others cared little how he looked – or how they looked, for that matter. For now they all spread out their

wings and rose in the air.
Of course you all know
what flying feels like
because everyone has
dreamed about flying, and it seems
so beautifully easy – only, you can
never remember how you did it. As
a rule you have
to do it without
wings in your
dreams, which is
more clever and
uncommon, but not so
easy to remember the rule for.
Now the four children rose
flapping from the ground, and you can't
think how good the air felt running

against their faces. Their wings were tremendously wide when they were spread out, and they had to fly quite a long way apart so as not to get in each other's way. But little things like this are easily learned.

All the words in the English Dictionary, and in the Greek Lexicon as well, are, I find, of no use at all to tell you exactly what it feels like to be flying, so I will not try. But I will say that to look down on the fields and woods, instead of along at them, is something like looking at a beautiful live map, where, instead of silly colours on paper, you have real moving sunny woods and green fields laid out one after the other. As Cyril said, and I can't think where he got hold of such a strange expression,

"It does you a fair treat!"

It was most wonderful and more like real magic than any wish the children had had yet…

The Greedy Brownie

Edited by Hamilton Wright Mabie,
Edward Everett Hale and
William Byron Forbush

*T*here was once a little Brownie who
lived in a hollow tree stump. He had been
busy all the day playing pranks, as all
Brownies love to do. His pranks had taken
him far away from home to the house of a
very important landowner, or laird. Into the
laird's cup of wine the Brownie had
dropped some horribly sour berries, which

he had picked on his way. The Brownie also put prickly thistles into the laird's boots, so that when he had drawn them on he had screamed out with pain.

The Brownie had been away all the day, so when at last he turned to go back to his home he felt really very tired. On his way back to the wood he passed by a cosy-looking farmhouse. The door of the dairy was open. The Brownie thought this would be a very nice cool place in which to rest for a few moments. So he slipped into the dairy and curled himself up underneath the bench to have a nice little doze.

He was so weary that once he had fallen asleep he never woke up again until it was quite dark. He was disturbed by two lassies who had come into the dairy. One was carrying a candle, and by its light the pair spied a big bowl of cream on the shelf. The naughty girls thought that they would drink it for supper. They could only find one spoon on the shelf, so they decided they would each have a spoonful in turn.

Lassie Jean carried the bowl to a bench in the corner, and Lassie Meg followed with the candle. No sooner had the two girls settled themselves than the Brownie, who was now wide awake and feeling that some supper might not be out of place, crept up behind them and blew out the candle.

The lassies at first were very concerned at being in the dark. Nevertheless, they determined they would drink the cream

all the same. Lassie Jean filled the spoon
with the rich delicacy. She was about to
raise it to her lips when the naughty
Brownie poked his head over her shoulder,
and lapped it out of
the spoon before
it had reached
her mouth.

Lassie Meg, believing that Lassie Jean had already swallowed some cream while she had had none, stretched out her hand to take away the spoon from her friend. Lassie Jean was not willing to give it up, since she said she had not yet tasted any cream.

Lassie Meg was unwilling to believe her, for she declared she had heard her lapping the cream. Without waiting for Lassie Jean to explain, she snatched the spoon from her friend's hand. She filled it with cream from the bowl, and was about to raise it to her lips when the Brownie jumped from behind Lassie Jean, and settled himself behind the shoulders of Lassie Meg. He poked forward his head, and again lapped up the cream from out of the spoon. Lassie Jean, in her

turn, snatched back the spoon from
Lassie Meg…

Thus they went on, for every time one
or the other raised the spoonful of cream
to her lips it was lapped up by the gleeful
Brownie. This continued until the bowl was
emptied. The Brownie was full of cream and
quite drunk with happiness, but the lassies
had not tasted one drop, although each
believed the other had drunk it all.

The foolish lassies were still quarrelling
when the door of the dairy was opened,
and the farmer's wife entered, carrying a
lighted candle in her hand. The moment
that she did so the tricksy Brownie hopped
underneath the bench, and the lassies
started up guiltily.

At once, the farmer's wife caught sight of the empty basin. She was very angry with the two girls indeed. When they tried hastily to explain, each blaming the other, the farmer's wife would not listen, but only grew the more angry. She told them that, since they had supped so well, they should have none of the scones and eggs which she had prepared for the evening meal.

When the farmer's wife had entered she had left the door open, so while she was busily scolding the lassies the naughty Brownie slipped out from under the bench and made his escape. As he ran chuckling down the road, he could still hear the farmer's wife's angry voice drowning the explanations of the bewildered lassies.

When the little fellow curled himself up some time later in the tree trunk he was still laughing.

Sillies and Simpletons

 Mr Vinegar

By Joseph Jacobs

Mr and Mrs Vinegar lived in a vinegar bottle. Now, one day, when Mr Vinegar was away from home, Mrs Vinegar (who was a very good housewife) was busily sweeping her house when an unlucky thump of the broom brought the whole house clitter-clatter, clitter-clatter about her ears. In an agony of grief she rushed forth to meet her husband.

Seeing him she exclaimed, "Oh, Mr Vinegar, Mr Vinegar, we are ruined. I have knocked the house down. It is all to pieces!"

Mr Vinegar then said, "My dear, let us see what can be done.

fair at the neighbouring town – you shall take these forty guineas and buy a cow. I can make butter and cheese, which you shall sell at the market, and we shall then be able to live very comfortably."

Mr Vinegar joyfully agreed. He took the money, and off he went to the fair. When he arrived he walked up and down, and at length saw a beautiful red cow. It was an excellent milker, and perfect in every way. 'Oh,' thought Mr Vinegar, 'if I had but that cow, I should be the happiest man alive.'

So he offered the forty guineas for the cow, and the owner said that, as he was a friend, he'd oblige him. So the bargain was made and Mr Vinegar got the cow, and he drove it backwards and forwards to show it.

By and by he saw a man playing the bagpipes, *tweedle-dum tweedle-dee.* The children followed him about, and he appeared to be pocketing money on all sides. 'Well,' thought Mr Vinegar, 'if I had but that beautiful instrument, I should be the happiest man alive – my fortune would be made.'

So Mr Vinegar went up to the man. "Friend," said he, "what a beautiful instrument that is, and what a deal of money you must make."

"Why, yes," said the man, "I make a great deal of money, to be sure, and it is a wonderful instrument."

"Oh!" cried Mr Vinegar, "how I should like to possess it!"

"Well," said the man, "as you are a friend, I don't much mind parting with it. You shall have it for that red cow."

"Done!" said the delighted Mr Vinegar. So the red cow was given for the bagpipes.

He walked up and down with his purchase, but it was in vain he tried to play a tune. Instead of pocketing pence, boys followed him hooting, laughing and throwing things.

Poor Mr Vinegar. His fingers grew very cold, and,

just as he was leaving the town, he met
a man with a fine thick pair of gloves.
"Oh, my fingers are so very cold," said
Mr Vinegar to himself. "Now if I had but
those beautiful gloves, I should be the
happiest man alive." He went up to the
man, and said to him, "Friend, you seem to
have a capital pair of gloves there."

"Yes, truly," cried the man, "and my
hands are as warm as possible this cold
November day."

"Well," said Mr Vinegar, "I should like to
have them."

"What will you give?" said the man. "As
you are a friend, I don't much mind letting
you have them for those bagpipes."

"Done!" cried Mr Vinegar. He put on the

gloves and felt perfectly happy as he trudged homewards.

At last he grew very tired, when he saw a man coming towards him with a good stout walking stick in his hand. "Oh," said Mr Vinegar, "that I had but that stick! I should then be the happiest man alive." He said to the man: "Friend! What a rare good stick you have got."

"Yes," said the man, "I have used it for many a long mile, and a good friend it has been. But if you have a fancy for it, as you are a friend, I don't mind giving it to you for that pair of gloves."

Mr Vinegar's hands were so warm, and his legs so tired, that he gladly made the exchange.

As he drew near to the wood where he had left his wife, he heard a parrot in a tree calling out his name.

"Mr Vinegar, you foolish man, you blockhead, you simpleton," mocked the parrot. "You went to the fair, and laid out all your money in buying a cow. Not content with that, you changed it for bagpipes, on which you could not play, and which were not worth one-tenth of the money. You had no sooner got the bagpipes than you changed them for gloves, which were not worth one-quarter of the money. And when you had got the gloves, you changed them for a poor miserable stick. And now for your forty guineas, cow, bagpipes and gloves, you have nothing to

show but that
miserable stick,
which you might
have cut in a hedge."

On this the bird
laughed, and
Mr Vinegar, falling
into a violent rage,
threw the stick at its
head. The stick
lodged in the tree,
and he returned to his wife without money,
cow, bagpipes, gloves or stick. She instantly
gave him such a sound scolding that he
never did anything quite so silly again.

The Moon-Cake

Edited by Hamilton Wright Mabie,
Edward Everett Hale and
William Byron Forbush

A little boy had a cake that a big boy really wanted for himself. The greedy lad thought hard, wondering how he could get the cake without making the little boy cry, for then surely it would attract his mother's attention and she would see what was going on. Just in time, as the little boy held up the cake to his lips to take a bite, the big boy hit on an idea.

"How much prettier that cake would be if it were more like the moon!" he remarked.

The little boy stopped, his mouth open wide, and examined the tasty morsel in his hand. 'Surely something that looked like the moon would indeed be prettier,' he thought to himself.

Seeing the little boy's hesitation, the big boy seized the chance to press on. "I can make it look like the moon," he promised, "I have done it many times before."

"Really?" asked the little boy. "Honest?"

"Of course," replied the big boy, with a smirk, "hand it over."

No sooner had the little boy handed over his delicious-looking cake than the big boy

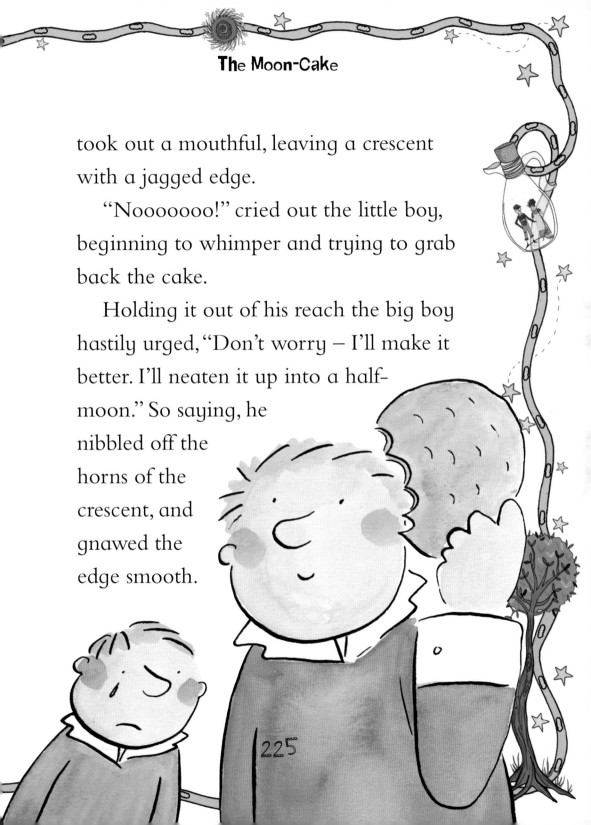

took out a mouthful, leaving a crescent with a jagged edge.

"Nooooooo!" cried out the little boy, beginning to whimper and trying to grab back the cake.

Holding it out of his reach the big boy hastily urged, "Don't worry – I'll make it better. I'll neaten it up into a half-moon." So saying, he nibbled off the horns of the crescent, and gnawed the edge smooth.

225

But when the half-moon was made, the little boy saw that there was hardly any cake left, and he began to wail. The big boy again interrupted, telling him that, if he did not like so small a moon, he should have one that was just the size of the real thing. He then took the cake, and explained that, just before the new moon is seen, the old moon disappears. Then he swallowed the rest of the cake and ran off, leaving the little boy waiting for the new moon.

The Remarkable Rocket

By Oscar Wilde

The King's son was going to be married,
so there was great rejoicing. He had waited
a whole year for his bride, and at last she
had arrived. She was a Russian princess,
and had driven all the way from Finland in
a sledge drawn by six reindeer. The sledge
was shaped like a great golden swan, and
between the swan's wings lay the Princess
herself. Her long ermine cloak reached

down to her feet, on her head was a tiny silver cap, and she was as pale as the Snow Palace in which she had always lived. As she drove through the streets all the people threw down flowers on her from the balconies.

At the gate of the castle the Prince was waiting to receive her. When he saw her he sank upon one knee, and kissed her hand. "Your picture was beautiful," he murmured, "but you are more beautiful than your picture." The Princess blushed.

When the day for the marriage arrived, it was a magnificent ceremony. The bride and bridegroom walked hand in hand under a canopy of purple velvet embroidered with little pearls. Then there

was a state banquet, which lasted for five hours. The Prince and Princess sat at the top of the Great Hall and drank out of a cup of clear crystal.

After the banquet there was a ball. The bride and bridegroom were to dance the Rose-dance together, and the King played the flute. He played very badly, but no one dared to tell him so because he was the King. Indeed, everybody cried out, "Charming! Charming!"

The last item on the programme was a grand display of fireworks, to be let off exactly at midnight. The little Princess had never seen a firework in her life and was most excited. At the end of the King's garden a great stand had been set up. As

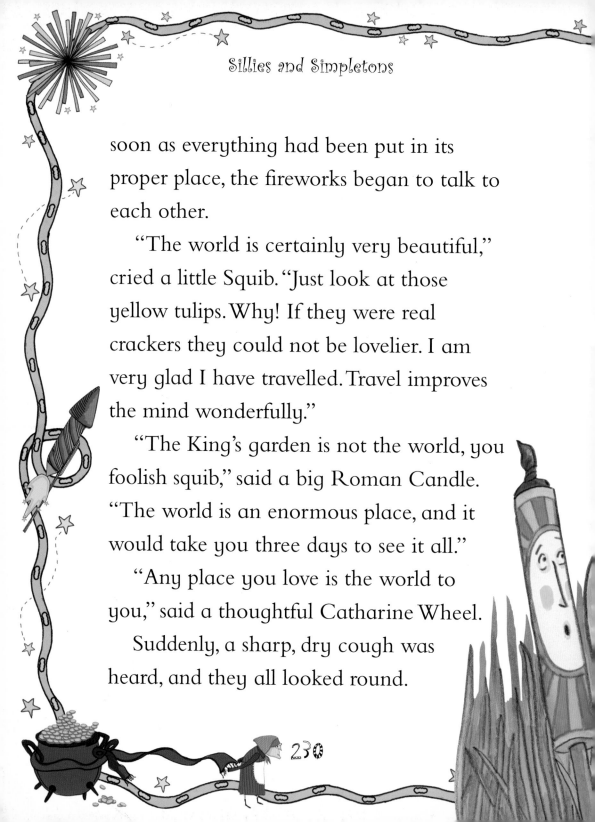

soon as everything had been put in its proper place, the fireworks began to talk to each other.

"The world is certainly very beautiful," cried a little Squib. "Just look at those yellow tulips. Why! If they were real crackers they could not be lovelier. I am very glad I have travelled. Travel improves the mind wonderfully."

"The King's garden is not the world, you foolish squib," said a big Roman Candle. "The world is an enormous place, and it would take you three days to see it all."

"Any place you love is the world to you," said a thoughtful Catharine Wheel.

Suddenly, a sharp, dry cough was heard, and they all looked round.

It came from a tall, haughty-looking
Rocket, who was tied to the end of
a long stick.

"Ahem! Ahem!" he said again. Then he spoke in a very distinguished manner. "How fortunate it is for the King's son," he remarked, "that he is to be married on the very day on which I am to be let off. Really, if it had been arranged beforehand, it could not have turned out better for him, but princes are always lucky."

"Dear me!" said the little Squib. "I thought it was quite the other way, and that we were to be let off in the Prince's honour."

"It may be so with you," he answered. "Indeed, I have no doubt that it is, but with me it is different. I am a very remarkable Rocket, and come of remarkable parents. My mother was the most celebrated

Catharine Wheel of her day, and was renowned for her graceful dancing. When she made her great public appearance she span round nineteen times before she went out, and each time that she did so she threw into the air seven pink stars. She was three feet and a half across, and made of the very best gunpowder.

"My father was a Rocket like myself," continued the Rocket, "and from French grandparents. He flew so high that the people were afraid that he would never come down again. He did though, and he made a most brilliant descent in a shower of golden rain. The newspapers wrote about his performance in very flattering terms. The *Court Gazette* called him a triumph!"

233

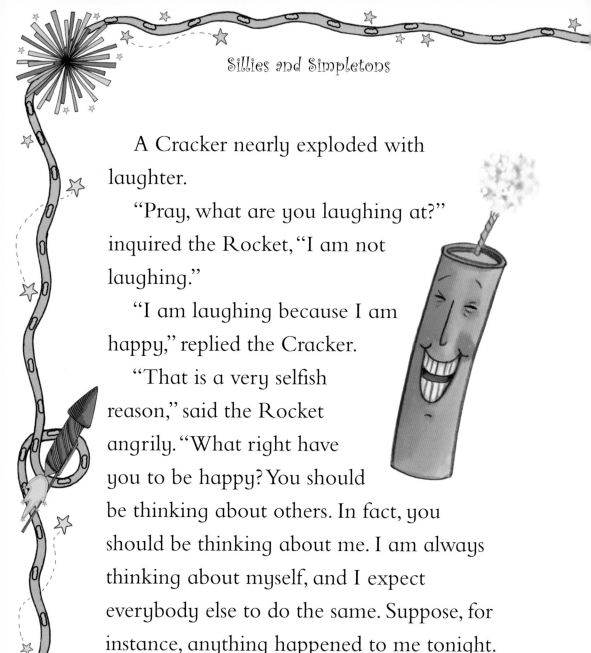

A Cracker nearly exploded with laughter.

"Pray, what are you laughing at?" inquired the Rocket, "I am not laughing."

"I am laughing because I am happy," replied the Cracker.

"That is a very selfish reason," said the Rocket angrily. "What right have you to be happy? You should be thinking about others. In fact, you should be thinking about me. I am always thinking about myself, and I expect everybody else to do the same. Suppose, for instance, anything happened to me tonight. What a misfortune that would be for

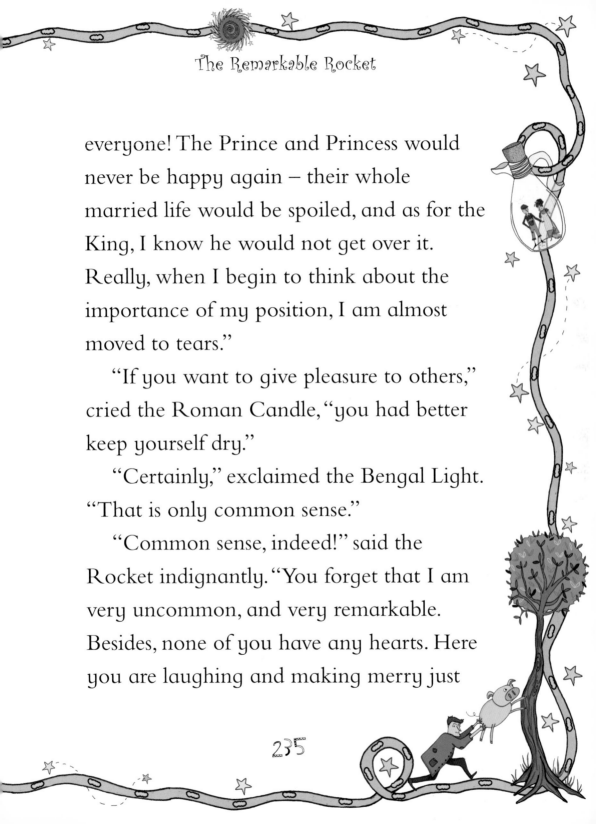

everyone! The Prince and Princess would never be happy again – their whole married life would be spoiled, and as for the King, I know he would not get over it. Really, when I begin to think about the importance of my position, I am almost moved to tears."

"If you want to give pleasure to others," cried the Roman Candle, "you had better keep yourself dry."

"Certainly," exclaimed the Bengal Light. "That is only common sense."

"Common sense, indeed!" said the Rocket indignantly. "You forget that I am very uncommon, and very remarkable. Besides, none of you have any hearts. Here you are laughing and making merry just as if the Prince and Princess had not just been married."

"Well, really," exclaimed a small Fire-balloon, "why not? It is a most joyful occasion, and when I soar up into the air I intend to tell the stars all about it. You will see them twinkle when I talk to them about the pretty bride."

"Ah! What a simple view of life!" said the Rocket. "But it is only what I expected. There is nothing in you – you are hollow and empty. Why, perhaps the Prince and Princess may go to live in a country where there is a deep river, and perhaps they may have only one son – a little fair-haired boy with violet eyes like the Prince himself, and perhaps some day he may go out to walk

with his nurse, and perhaps the nurse may go to sleep under a great elder tree, and perhaps the little boy may fall into the deep river and be drowned. What a terrible misfortune! Poor people, to lose their only son! It is really too dreadful! I shall never get over it."

"But they have not lost their only son," said the Roman Candle. "No misfortune has happened to them at all."

"I never said that they had," replied the Rocket. "I said that they might. If they had lost their only son there would be no use in saying anything more about the matter. I hate people who cry over spilt milk. But when I think that they might lose their only son, I certainly am very much affected."

"You certainly are!" cried the Bengal
Light. "In fact, you are the most affected
person I ever met."

"You are the rudest person I ever met,"
said the Rocket, quite offended, "and
you cannot understand my friendship
for the Prince."

"You had really better keep
yourself dry," said the Fire-balloon.
"That is the important thing."

"Very important for you, I have
no doubt," answered the Rocket,
"but I shall weep if I choose."
And he actually burst into real
tears, which flowed down his
stick like raindrops. They
nearly drowned two little

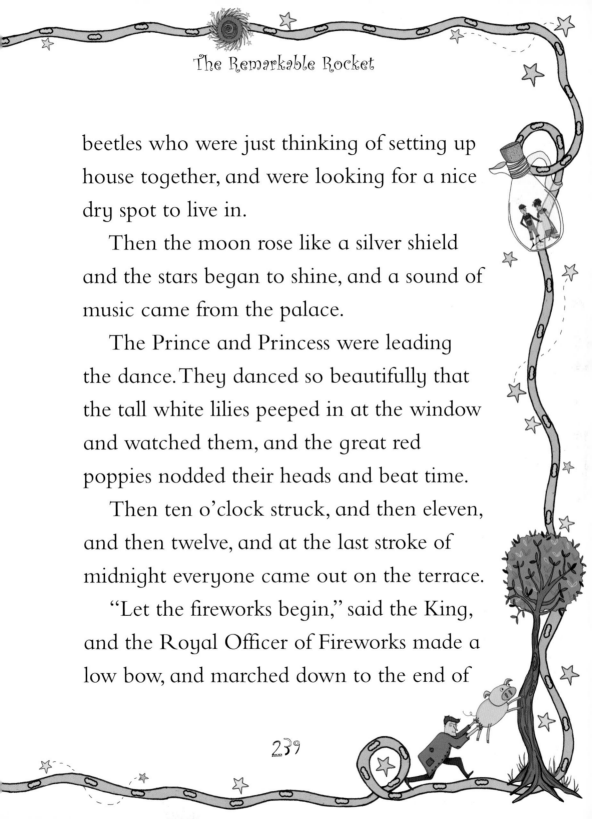

beetles who were just thinking of setting up house together, and were looking for a nice dry spot to live in.

Then the moon rose like a silver shield and the stars began to shine, and a sound of music came from the palace.

The Prince and Princess were leading the dance. They danced so beautifully that the tall white lilies peeped in at the window and watched them, and the great red poppies nodded their heads and beat time.

Then ten o'clock struck, and then eleven, and then twelve, and at the last stroke of midnight everyone came out on the terrace.

"Let the fireworks begin," said the King, and the Royal Officer of Fireworks made a low bow, and marched down to the end of the garden. He had six attendants with him, each of whom carried a lighted torch at the end of a long pole.

It was certainly a magnificent display.

Whizz! Whizz! went the Catharine Wheel, as she spun round and round. *Boom! Boom!* went the Roman Candle. Then the Squibs danced all over the place, and the Bengal Lights made everything look scarlet. "Goodbye," cried the Fire-balloon, as he soared away dropping tiny blue sparks. *Bang! Bang!* answered the Crackers, who were enjoying themselves immensely. Every one was a great success, except the Remarkable Rocket. He was so damp with crying that he could not go off at all. The best thing in him was the gunpowder, and

that was so wet with tears that it was of no use. All his poor relations, to whom he would never speak, except with a sneer, shot up into the sky like wonderful golden flowers with blossoms of fire.

"Huzza! Huzza!" cried the court, and the little Princess laughed with pleasure.

"I suppose they are reserving me for some grand occasion," said the Rocket, "no doubt that is what it means," and he looked more haughty than ever as the ball finished.

The next day the workmen came to put everything tidy. "This is evidently a welcome party sent for me," said the Rocket to himself, "I will receive them with suitable dignity." So he put his nose in the air, and began to frown severely as if he were thinking about some very important subject. But they took no notice of him at all till they were just going away. Then one of them caught sight of him. "Hallo!" he cried, "What a bad rocket!" and he threw him over the wall into the ditch.

"*Bad* Rocket? *Bad* Rocket?" said the Rocket as he whirled through the air. "Impossible! *Grand* Rocket, that is what the man said. *Bad* and *grand* sound very much the same, indeed they often are the same," and he fell into the mud. "It is not comfortable here," he remarked, "but no doubt it is some fashionable health spa, and they have sent me to improve my health. My nerves are certainly very much shattered, and I need rest."

After some time a large white duck swam by. She had yellow legs and webbed feet, and was considered a great beauty on account of her waddle.

"Quack, quack, quack," she said. "What a curious shape you are! Were you born like that, or is it the result of an accident?"

"It is quite evident that you have always lived in the country," answered the Rocket, "otherwise you would know who I am. However, I will excuse your ignorance. It would be unfair to expect other people to be as remarkable as oneself. You will no doubt be surprised to hear that I can fly up into the sky, and come down in a shower of golden rain."

"I don't think much of that," said the Duck, "as I cannot see what use it is to anyone. Now, if you could plough the fields like the ox, or draw a cart like the horse, or look after the sheep like the collie dog, that would be something."

"My good creature," cried the Rocket in a very haughty tone of voice, "a person of

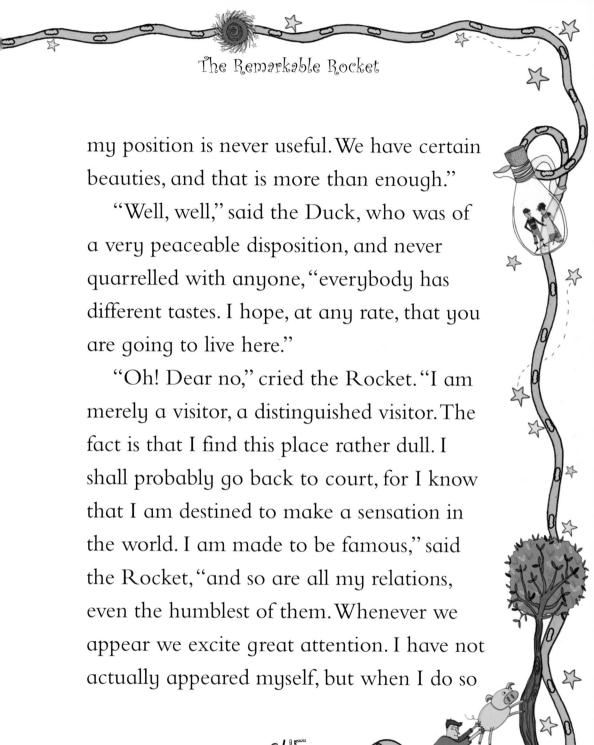

my position is never useful. We have certain beauties, and that is more than enough."

"Well, well," said the Duck, who was of a very peaceable disposition, and never quarrelled with anyone, "everybody has different tastes. I hope, at any rate, that you are going to live here."

"Oh! Dear no," cried the Rocket. "I am merely a visitor, a distinguished visitor. The fact is that I find this place rather dull. I shall probably go back to court, for I know that I am destined to make a sensation in the world. I am made to be famous," said the Rocket, "and so are all my relations, even the humblest of them. Whenever we appear we excite great attention. I have not actually appeared myself, but when I do so it will be a magnificent sight."

"Ah! The higher things of life, how fine they are!" said the Duck. "And that reminds me how hungry I feel." And she swam away down the stream, saying, "Quack, quack, quack."

"Come back! Come back!" screamed the Rocket. "I have a great deal to say to you," but the Duck paid no attention to him.

He sank a little deeper still into the mud, when suddenly two little boys in white smocks came running down the bank with a kettle and a bundle of sticks for making a fire. "Hello!" cried one of the boys. "Look at this old stick! I wonder how it came here," and he picked the rocket out of the ditch.

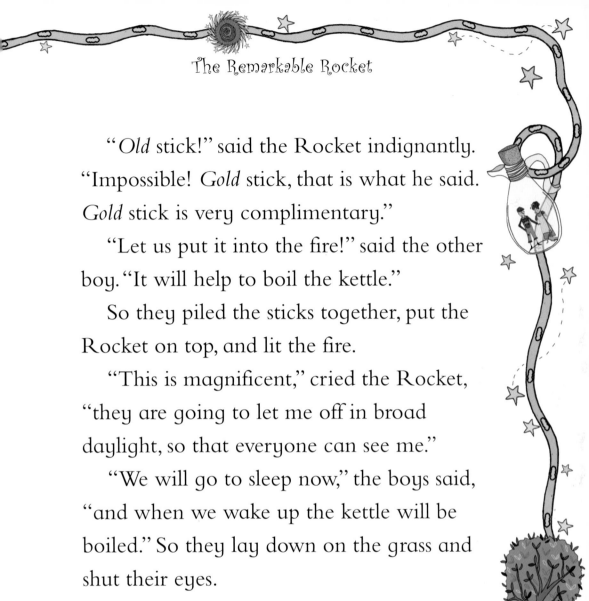

"*Old* stick!" said the Rocket indignantly. "Impossible! *Gold* stick, that is what he said. *Gold* stick is very complimentary."

"Let us put it into the fire!" said the other boy. "It will help to boil the kettle."

So they piled the sticks together, put the Rocket on top, and lit the fire.

"This is magnificent," cried the Rocket, "they are going to let me off in broad daylight, so that everyone can see me."

"We will go to sleep now," the boys said, "and when we wake up the kettle will be boiled." So they lay down on the grass and shut their eyes.

The Rocket was very damp, so he took a long time to burn. At last, however, the fire caught him.

"Now I am going off!" he cried, and he made himself very stiff and straight. "I know I shall go much higher than the stars, much higher than the moon, much higher than the sun. In fact, I shall go so high that—"

Fizz! Fizz! Fizz! and he went straight up into the air.

"Delightful!" he cried. "I shall go on like this forever. What a success I am!"

But nobody saw him.

Then he began to feel a curious tingling sensation all over him.

"Now I am going to explode," he cried. "I shall set the whole world on fire and make such a noise that nobody will talk about anything else for a year."

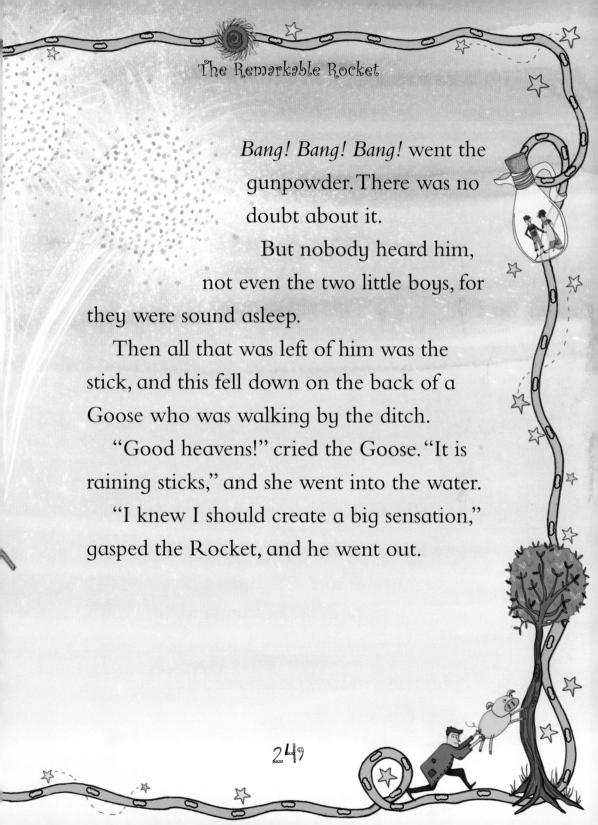

Bang! Bang! Bang! went the gunpowder. There was no doubt about it.

But nobody heard him, not even the two little boys, for they were sound asleep.

Then all that was left of him was the stick, and this fell down on the back of a Goose who was walking by the ditch.

"Good heavens!" cried the Goose. "It is raining sticks," and she went into the water.

"I knew I should create a big sensation," gasped the Rocket, and he went out.

His eyes gleaming with excitement, the King tore off the paper and saw that there was… nothing in the weaver's outstretched, flat palms. All the viziers and nobles who stood there looked at the weaver's hands and, instead of seeing a folded length of gloriously woven material ready to be wound into a turban, saw *nothing*.

The King's face fell and he said in his heart, 'Oh my goodness! I must be a fool!' He was absolutely crushed!

Then straight away he thought, 'But I have no choice — I will have to pretend! I will have to say it is a wonderful turban and admire it, or else I will be put to shame before everybody. All my servants and subjects will know that I have been shown to be an idiot!' So he forced himself to smile and say, "Oh it is a wonderful turban, I like it very much."

Then the weaver said, "O King, let them bring a cap that I may wind the turban for you." They

253

brought a cap and put it on the King's head, and the weaver moved his hands as though he wound the turban.

All the nobles who were standing there said, "Blessed be it! O King, how fair, how beautiful a turban!" and they applauded it with great enthusiasm.

The King swallowed hard. He summoned his two closest advisors to accompany him into a private room and locked the door. Then he span round and hissed, "O viziers, I must be the world's greatest fool, for I cannot see the turban!"

The viziers looked at each other, then back at the king, and admitted, "O King, we too can't see it!"

Then all three rushed to unlock the door,

so they could catch the weaver and have him thrown into the deepest, darkest dungeon. But of course – the weaver was gone, out of the palace, off into the narrow streets of the city, vanished without a trace – taking all the money the King had paid along with him.

The Hedley Kow

By Joseph Jacobs

There was once an old woman who earned a poor living by running errands and suchlike for the farmers' wives round about the village where she lived. It wasn't much she earned by it, but with a plate of meat at one house and a cup of tea at another, she managed to get by somehow, and always looked as cheerful as if she hadn't a want in the world.

Well, one summer evening as the old woman was trotting away homewards, she came upon a big, black pot lying at the side of the road.

"Now that," said she, stopping to look at it, "would be just the very thing for me if I had anything to put into it! But who could have left it here?" and she looked round about, as if the person it belonged to must be not far off. But she could see no one.

"Maybe it'll have a hole in it," she said thoughtfully. "Ay, that'll be why they've left it lying. But then it'd do fine to put a flower in for the window, I'm thinking I'll just take it home anyways." And she bent her stiff old back, and lifted the lid to look inside.

"Mercy me!" she cried, and jumped

257

back to the other side of the road. "If it isn't full to the brim o' gold pieces!"

For a while she could do nothing but walk round and round her treasure, admiring the yellow gold and wondering at her good luck, and saying to herself about

252

every two minutes, "Well, I do be feeling rich and grand!" But presently she began to think how she could best take it home with her. She couldn't see any other way than by fastening one end of her shawl to it and dragging it after her along the road.

"It'll certainly be dark soon," she said to herself, "and folk'll not see what I'm bringing home with me, and so I'll have all the night to myself to think what I'll do with it. I could buy a grand house and all, and live like the Queen herself, and not do a stroke of work all day, but just sit by the fire with a cup of tea. Or maybe I'll give it to the priest to keep for me, and get a piece whenever I want. Or maybe I'll just bury it in a hole at the bottom of the garden, and put one gold piece on the chimney, between the china teapot and the spoons – for ornament like. Ah! I feel so grand, I don't know myself!"

By this time, being already rather tired with dragging such a heavy weight after her, the old woman stopped to rest for a minute, turning to make sure that her treasure was safe.

But when she looked back at it, it wasn't a pot of gold at all, but a great lump of shining silver!

She stared at it, and rubbed her eyes and stared at it again, but she couldn't make it look like anything but a great lump of silver. "I'd have sworn it was a pot of gold," she said at last, "but I reckon I must have

been dreaming. Ay, now, that's a change for the better. It'll be far less trouble to look after, and not so easily stolen. Those gold pieces would have been a lot of bother to keep safe anyway. Ay, I'm well quit of them, and with my bonny lump I'm as rich as rich!"

She set off homewards again, cheerfully planning all the grand things she was going to do with her money. It wasn't very long, however, before she got tired again and so she stopped once more to rest for a minute or two.

Again she turned to look at her treasure, and as soon as she set eyes on it she cried out in astonishment, "Oh, my!" said she, "now it's a lump o' iron! Well, that beats all,

as big as a great horse. Then it threw
down four lanky legs and shook
out two long ears,
flourished a tail, and
went off kicking its
feet into the air and
laughing like a
naughty, mocking boy.

   The old woman stared
after it, till it was fairly out
of sight.

   "*Well!*" she said at last, "I
do be the luckiest body hereabouts!
I'd heard of that magical Hedley
Kow that plays tricks on unsuspecting
folk, but I never dreamed I would see
it with my own eyes, all to myself!

264

I can tell you, I do feel
that *grand*!"
And she went into her cottage,
and sat down by the fire
to think over her
good luck.

The Six Sillies

By Andrew Lang

Once upon a time there was a young girl who reached the age of thirty-seven without ever having had a lover, for she was so foolish that no one wanted to marry her.

However, one day a young man arrived to pay his respects to her and her parents. Beaming with joy, her mother sent her daughter down to the cellar to draw a jug of beer.

As the girl never came back the mother

went down to see what had become of her. She found her sitting on the stairs, her head in her hands, while by her side the beer was running all over the floor as she had forgotten to close the tap. "What are you doing there?" asked the mother.

"I was thinking what I shall call my first child after I am married to that young man. All the best names are taken already by others in the village."

The mother sat down on the staircase

267

beside her daughter and said, "I will think about it with you, my dear."

The father, who had stayed upstairs with the young man, was surprised that neither his wife nor his daughter came back, and in turn went down to look for them. He found them both sitting on the stairs, while beside them the beer was running all over the ground from the tap, which was open.

"What are you doing there? The beer is running all over the cellar."

"We were thinking what we should call the children that our daughter will have when she marries that young man. All the best names are taken," replied the mother.

"Well," said the father, "I will think about it with you."

As neither mother nor daughter nor father came upstairs again, the young man grew impatient, and went down into the cellar to see what they could all be doing. He found them all three sitting on the stairs, while beside them the beer was running all over the ground from the tap, which was wide open.

"What in the world are you all doing that you don't come upstairs, and that you let the beer run all over the cellar?"

"Yes, I know, my boy," said the father, "but if you marry our daughter what shall you call your children? All the best names are already taken."

When the young man heard this answer he replied, "Well! Goodbye, I am going

away. When I have found three people sillier than you I will come back and marry your daughter."

So he continued his journey, and after walking a long way he reached an orchard. There he saw some people knocking down walnuts, and trying to throw them into a cart with a fork.

"What are you doing there?" he asked.

"We want to load the cart with our walnuts, but we can't manage to do it."

The young man advised them to get a basket and to put the walnuts in it, so as to turn them into the cart.

"Well," the young man said to himself, "I have already found someone more foolish than those three."

So he went on his way, and
he came to a wood. There he
saw a man who wanted to
give his pig some acorns
to eat, and was
trying with all his
might to make
him climb up the
oak tree.

"What are you
doing, my good man?" asked he.

"I want to make my pig eat
some acorns, but I can't get
him to go up the tree,"
replied the man.

"If you climb up and
shake down the acorns

the pig would pick them up and eat them."

"Oh, I never thought of that."

"Here is the second idiot," said the young man to himself.

Some way farther along the road he came upon a man who had never worn any trousers, and who was trying to put on a pair. So he had fastened them to a tree, and was jumping with all his might up in the air so that he should hit the two legs of the trousers as he came down.

"It would be much better if you held them in your hands," said the young man, "and then put your legs one after the other in each hole."

"Dear me, to be sure! You are sharper than I am, for that never occurred to me."

272

So having found three people more
foolish than his bride, or her father, or her
mother, the young man went back to marry
the young lady.

And in course of time they had a great
many children.

Day-Dreaming

By Joseph Jacobs

Now there was once a man of Bagdad who had seven sons, and when he died he left to each of them one hundred dirhems.

His fifth son, called Alnaschar the Babbler, spent all this money on a precious vase, and he put it in a big tray from which to show and sell it. He sat down on a raised bench at the foot of a wall, against which he leaned back, placing the tray on the ground in front of him.

Day-Dreaming

As he sat he began day-dreaming, and said to himself, "I have spent a hundred dirhems on this vase. Now I will surely sell it for two hundred, and with that I will buy more vases and sell them for four hundred, and I will not cease to buy and sell till I become master of much wealth. With this I will buy all kinds of luxuries and jewels and perfumes, and make great profit on them till, God willing, I will have a hundred thousand dinars or two million dirhems. Then I will buy a handsome house, together with servants and horses and trappings of gold, and I will eat and drink and be merry."

This he said looking at the tray before him with a vase worth a hundred dirhems.

Then he continued, "When I have amassed a hundred thousand dinars I will demand the hand of the Vizier's daughter in marriage, for I hear that she is perfect in beauty. When I return home, I will hire ten little servants, and clothes for myself such as those worn by kings and sultans, and get a saddle of gold set thick with precious jewels.

Then I will mount my horse and parade the city, with servants before and behind me, while the people will salute me and call down blessings upon me.

"Then I will go to the Vizier, the girl's father, with servants behind and before me, as well as on either hand. When the Vizier sees me, he will rise and seat me in his own place, while he himself sits down below me, because I am his son-in-law. I will have with me two servants with purses, and I will offer him a present of a thousand dinars so that he may recognize my nobility, generosity and greatness of mind, and for every ten words he will say to me, I will answer him only two.

"Then I will return to my house. If

but will sit by her without looking, so that she may say I am a good man with a pure soul. Her mother will come to me and kiss my head and hands, and say to me, 'O my lord, look on your bride, for she longs for your favour.'

"Then she will fetch a cup of wine, and her daughter will take it and come to me, but I will leave her standing while I lay back upon a cushion. I will not look at her, so that she will think me to be a sultan of great dignity. She will say to me, 'O my lord, for God's sake, do not refuse to take this cup, for indeed I am yours.' But I will not speak to her, and she will press me, saying, 'Please, drink,' and put it to my lips. Then I will shake my fist and push her away with my foot, so…"

So saying, Alnaschar gave a kick with his foot and knocked over the vase, which fell over and was broken to bits.

The Simpleton

By Andrew Lang

Once upon a time there lived a man who was as rich as he could be, but as no happiness in this world is ever quite complete, he had an only son who was such a simpleton that he could barely add two and two together. At last his father determined to put up with his stupidity no longer and, giving him a purse full of gold, sent him to seek his fortune in foreign lands, telling him to be mindful of the saying:

'How much a fool that's sent to roam
Excels a fool that stays at home.'

Moscione, for this was the youth's name,
mounted a horse and set out for Venice,
hoping to find a ship there that would take
him to Cairo. After he had ridden for some
time he saw a man standing at the foot of a
poplar tree, and said to him, "What's your
name, my friend? Where do you come from,
and what can you do?"

The man replied, "My name is Quick-
as-Thought and I come from Fleet-town. I
can run like lightning."

"I should like to see you," returned
Moscione.

"Just wait a minute, then," said

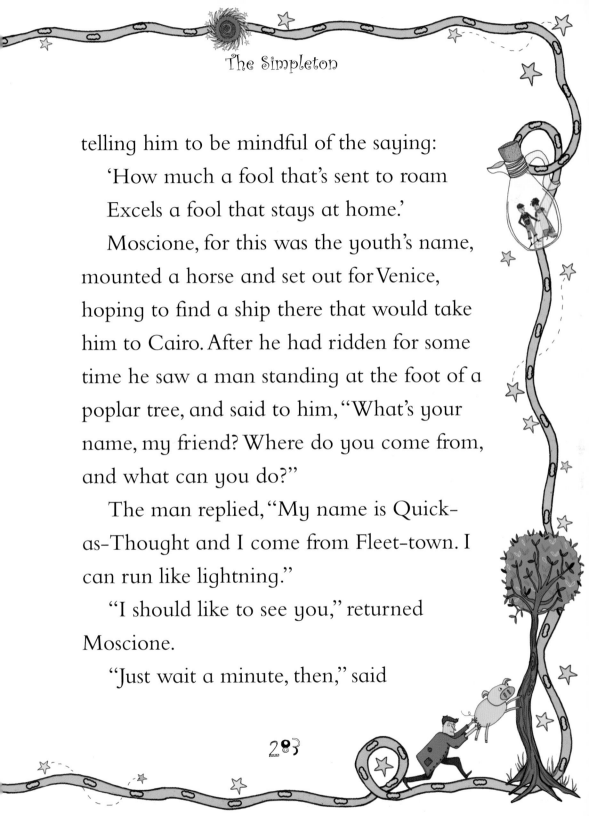

Quick-as-Thought, "and I will soon show you that I am speaking the truth."

The words were hardly out of his mouth when a young doe ran right across the field they were standing in.

Quick-as-Thought let her run on a short distance, in order to give her a start, and then pursued her so quickly and so lightly that you could not have tracked his footsteps if the field had been strewn with flour. In a few springs he had overtaken

274

the doe. He had so impressed Moscione
with his fleetness of foot that he begged
Quick-as-Thought to go with him,
promising at the same time to reward him
handsomely.

Quick-as-Thought agreed to his
proposal, and they continued on their
journey together. They had hardly gone a
mile when they met a young man,
and Moscione stopped and
asked him, "What's your name,
my friend? Where do you come
from, and what can you do?"
The man answered promptly,
"I am called Hare's-Ear and I come
from Curiosity Valley. If I lay my
ear on the ground, without

moving from the spot, I can hear everything that goes on in the world – the plots and gossip of court and cottage, and all the plans of mice and men."

"If that's the case," replied Moscione, "tell me what's going on in my own home at present."

The youth laid his ear to the ground and at once reported, "An old man is saying to his wife, 'Heaven be praised that we have got rid of Moscione, for perhaps, when he has been out in the world a little, he may gain some common sense, and return home less of a fool than when he set out'."

"Enough, enough," cried Moscione. "You speak the truth, and I believe you. Come with us and your fortune's made."

The young man consented, and after they had gone about ten miles, they met a third man, to whom Moscione said, "What's your name, my brave fellow? Where were you born, and what can you do?"

The man replied, "I am called Hit-the-Point, I come from the city of Perfect-aim, and I draw my bow so exactly that I can shoot a pea off a stone."

"I should like to see you do it, if you've no objection," said Moscione.

The man at once placed a pea on a stone, and, drawing his bow, he shot it through the middle with the greatest possible ease.

When Moscione saw that the man had spoken the truth, he immediately asked

Hit-the-Point to join his party.

After they had all travelled together for some days, they came upon a number of people who were digging a trench in the blazing sun. Moscione felt so sorry for them that he said, "My dear friends, how can you stand working so hard in heat that would cook an egg in a minute?"

But one of the workmen answered, "We are as fresh as daisies, for we have a young man among us who blows on our backs like the west wind."

"Let me see him," said Moscione.

The youth was called, and Moscione asked him, "What's your name? Where do you come from, and what can you do?"

He answered, "I am called Blow-Blast. I

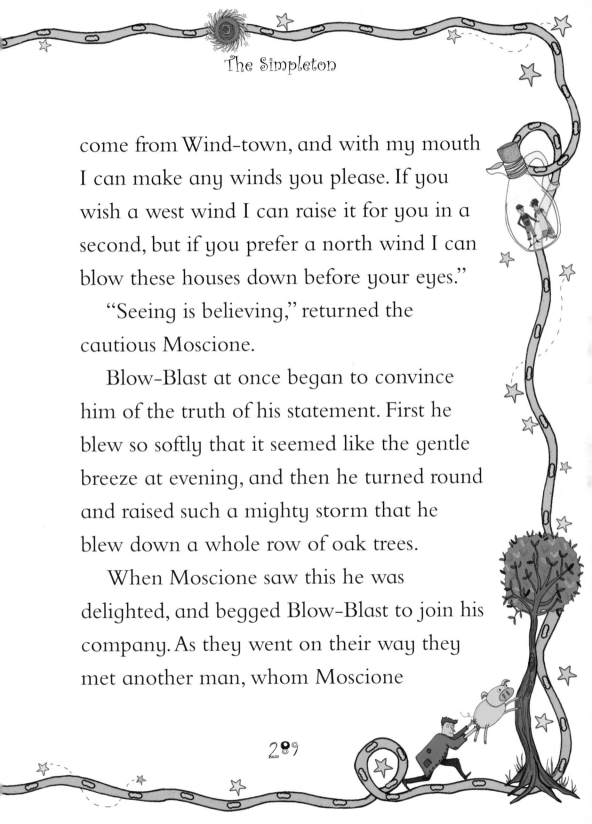

come from Wind-town, and with my mouth I can make any winds you please. If you wish a west wind I can raise it for you in a second, but if you prefer a north wind I can blow these houses down before your eyes."

"Seeing is believing," returned the cautious Moscione.

Blow-Blast at once began to convince him of the truth of his statement. First he blew so softly that it seemed like the gentle breeze at evening, and then he turned round and raised such a mighty storm that he blew down a whole row of oak trees.

When Moscione saw this he was delighted, and begged Blow-Blast to join his company. As they went on their way they met another man, whom Moscione addressed as usual, "What's your name? Where do you come from, and what can you do?"

"I am called Strong-Back. I come from Power-borough. I possess such strength that I can take a mountain on my back and it seems a feather to me," the man replied.

"If that's the case," said Moscione, "I should like some proof of your strength."

Then Strong-Back loaded himself with great boulders and tree trunks, so that a hundred waggons could not have taken away all that he carried on his back.

When Moscione saw this he persuaded Strong-Back to join his troop, and they all continued on their journey till they came to a country called Flower Vale.

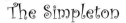

Here there reigned a king whose only daughter could run as quickly as the wind, and so lightly that she could run over a field of young oats without bending a single blade. The King had given out a proclamation that anyone who could beat the Princess in a race should have her for a wife, but that all who failed should lose their head.

As soon as Moscione heard of the royal proclamation, he hurried to see the King and challenged the Princess to race with him. But on the morning appointed for the trial he sent word to the King that he was not feeling well, and that as he could not run himself he would supply someone to take his place.

281

"It's just the same to me," said Canetella, the Princess. "Let anyone come forward that likes. I am quite prepared to meet him."

At the time appointed for the race the whole place was crowded with lots of people anxious to see the contest. Punctual to the moment, Quick-as-Thought and Canetella who was dressed in a short skirt and very light shoes appeared at the starting point.

Then a silver trumpet sounded. The two rivals started on their race, looking for all the world like a greyhound chasing a hare.

But Quick-as-Thought, true to his name, outran the Princess, and when the goal was reached, the people all clapped their hands and shouted, "Long live the stranger!"

Canetella was very fed up at being beaten, but, as the race had to be run a second time, she determined she would not be bested again. Accordingly, she went home and sent Quick-as-Thought a magic ring. It prevented the person who wore it not only from running, but even from walking. The Princess begged that he would wear it for her sake.

Early next morning the crowd assembled on the racecourse, and Canetella and Quick-as-Thought began their trial afresh. The Princess ran as quickly as ever, but poor Quick-as-Thought was like an overloaded donkey, and could not go a step.

Hit-the-Point had heard all about the Princess's trick from Hare's-Ear. When he saw the danger his friend was in, he seized his bow and arrow and, with perfect aim, shot the stone out of the ring that Quick-as-Thought was wearing. In a moment the youth's legs became free again, and in five bounds he had overtaken Canetella and won the race.

The King was much disgusted when he saw that he must acknowledge Moscione as his future son-in-law, and summoned the wise men of his court to ask if there was no way out of the difficulty.

The council at once decided that

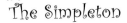

Canetella was far too dainty a girl to become the wife of such a travelling tinker. They advised the King to offer Moscione a present of gold, which no doubt a beggar like him would prefer to all the wives in the world.

The King was delighted at this suggestion. He called Moscione before him and asked him what sum of money he would take instead of his promised bride.

Moscione first consulted with his friends, and then answered, "I demand as much gold and precious stones as my followers can carry away."

The King thought he was being let off very easily. He produced coffers of gold, sacks of silver, and chests of precious stones,

but the more Strong-Back was loaded with
the treasure the straighter he stood.

At last the treasury was quite exhausted.
The King had to send his courtiers to his
subjects to collect all the gold and silver
they possessed. But nothing was of any
avail, and Strong-Back only asked for more.

When the King's counsellors saw the
unexpected result of their advice, they said
it would be more than foolish to let some
strolling thieves take so much treasure out of
the country, and urged the King to send
soldiers after them.

So the King sent a body of armed men
on foot and horse to take back the treasure
Strong-Back was carrying away with him.

But Hare's-Ear had heard what the

counsellors had advised the King and told his companions just as the dust of their pursuers was visible on the horizon.

No sooner had Blow-Blast taken in their danger than he raised such a mighty wind that all the King's army was blown down like nine-pins. As they were unable to get up again, Moscione and his companions went on their way without further ado.

As soon as they reached his home, Moscione divided his spoil with his companions. He stayed with his father, who was forced to admit at last that his son was not such a fool as he looked.

A Visitor from Paradise

By Joseph Jacobs

There was once a woman, good but simple, whose first husband died, so she married again. One day, when her second husband was out working in the fields, a weary tramp came trudging by her door and asked for a drink of water. When she handed it to him, and being rather a gossip,

299

Then the woman said, "There's our old Dobbin in the stable. I can't lend you mare Juniper 'cause my husband's ploughing with her just now."

"Ah, well, Dobbin'll do as it's only until tomorrow."

The woman got out Dobbin and saddled him, and the man took the clothes, pipe and beer, then rode off with them.

Shortly afterwards the woman's husband came

302

home and said, "What's become of Dobbin? He's not in the stable."

So his wife told him all that had happened. He said, "I don't like that. How do we know that he is going to paradise? How do we know that he'll bring Dobbin back tomorrow? I'll saddle Juniper and get our things back. Which way did he go?"

So her husband saddled Juniper and rode after the man, who saw him coming afar off and guessed what had happened. So he got off from Dobbin and drove him into a clump of trees near the roadside, and then went and laid down on his back and looked up to the sky. When the farmer came up to him, he got down from Juniper and said, "What are you doing there?"

"Oh, such a funny thing," said the man. "A fellow came along here on a horse with some clothes and things, and when he got to the top of the hill here he simply gave a shout and the horse went right up into the sky. I was watching him just now when you came up."

"Oh, it's all right then," said the farmer. "He's gone to paradise, sure enough," and went back to his wife.

Next day they waited, and they waited for the man to bring back Dobbin, but he didn't come that day nor the next day, nor the next.

And they are still waiting.

The Blind Men and the Elephant

By James Baldwin

There were once six blind men who stood by the roadside every day, and scraped out a living by begging from the people who passed. They knew that all sorts of sights passed them by, for they heard all the talk of the travellers who went up and down the road. But they had never seen anything, for being blind, how could they?

It so happened one morning that an

elephant was driven down the road where they stood. When they were told that such a great beast was before them, they asked the driver to let him stop so that they might see him.

Of course they could not see him with their eyes, but they thought that by touching him they could learn just what kind of animal he was.

The first one happened to put his hand on the elephant's side. "Well, well!" he said. "Now I know all about this beast. He is exactly like a wall."

The second felt only of the elephant's tusk. "My brother," he said, "you are mistaken. He is not at all like a wall. He is round and smooth and sharp. He is more like a spear than anything else."

The third happened to take hold of the elephant's trunk. "Both of you are wrong," he said. "Anybody who knows anything can see that this elephant is like a snake."

The fourth reached out his arms, and grasped one of the elephant's legs. "Oh, how blind you are!" he said. "It is very plain to me that he is round and tall like a tree."

The fifth chanced to take hold of the elephant's ear. "The blindest man ought to know that this beast is not like any of the things that you name," he said. "He is just like a huge fan."

The sixth was very blind indeed, and it was some time before he could find the elephant at all. At last he seized the animal's tail. "O foolish fellows!" he cried. "You

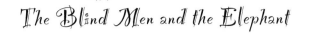

surely have lost your senses. This elephant is not like a wall, or a spear, or a snake, or a tree, neither is he like a fan. But any man with a particle of sense can see that he is exactly like a rope."

Then the elephant moved on, and the six blind men sat by the roadside all day, and quarrelled about it. Each believed that he knew just how the animal looked, and each called the others names because they did not agree with him.

People who have eyes sometimes act just as foolishly.

Baffled Beasts
and
Bamboozled Birds

The Open Road

An extract from *The Wind in the Willows*
by Kenneth Grahame

*The Mole has just moved into a new home at the riverbank
when he makes friends with the Water Rat, who introduces him
to the joy of messing around in boats…*

"Ratty," said Mole, "what I wanted to ask
you was, won't you take me to call on
Mr Toad? I've heard so much about him,
and I would like to make his acquaintance."
"Why, certainly," said the good-natured

Rat, jumping to his feet. "Get the boat out, and we'll paddle up there at once. It's never the wrong time to call on Toad. Early or late, he's always the same fellow. Always good-tempered, always glad to see you, always sorry when you go!"

"He must be a very nice animal," observed the Mole, as he got into the boat and took the sculls, while the Rat settled himself comfortably in the stern.

"He is indeed the best of animals," replied Rat. "So simple, so good-natured, and so affectionate. Perhaps he's not very clever – we can't all be geniuses – and it may be that he is both boastful and conceited. But he has got some great qualities, has Toady."

Rounding a bend in the river, they came in sight of a handsome, dignified old house of mellowed red brick, with well-kept lawns reaching down to the water's edge.

"There's Toad Hall," said the Rat.

They glided up the creek, and the Mole slipped his sculls as they passed into the shadow of a large boathouse. Here they saw many handsome boats, but none in the water. The place had an unused and deserted air.

The Rat looked around him. "I understand," said he. "Boating is played out. He's tired of it and done with it. I wonder what new fad he has taken up now?"

They disembarked and strolled across the flower-decked lawns in search of Toad,

whom they presently
happened upon resting in
a wicker garden chair,
with a preoccupied
expression on his
face, and a large
map spread out
on his knees.

"Hooray!" he
cried, jumping up on
seeing them. "This is splendid!" He shook
the paws of both of them warmly, never
waiting for an introduction to the Mole. "I
need both of you – badly! You've got to
help me. It's most important!"

"It's about your rowing, I suppose," said
the Rat. "You're getting on fairly well,

though you splash a good bit still. With a great deal of patience, and any quantity of coaching, you may—"

"Oh, pooh! Boating!" interrupted the Toad, in great disgust. "Silly boyish amusement. I've given that up *long* ago. Waste of time, that's what it is. No, I've discovered the real thing. Come with me, and you shall see what you shall see!"

He led the way to the stable yard, the Rat following with a most mistrustful expression. There, drawn out of the coach house into the open, they saw a gypsy caravan, shining with newness, painted a canary-yellow picked out with green, and red wheels.

"There you are!" cried the Toad, puffing out his chest with pride. "There's real life for you, embodied in that little cart. The open road, the dusty highway, the heath, the common, the hedgerows, the rolling downs! Camps, villages, towns, cities! Here today, up and off to somewhere else tomorrow! Travel, change, interest, excitement! The whole world before you, and a horizon that's always changing! And mind – this is the very finest cart of its sort that was ever built, without any exception! Come inside and look at the arrangements. Planned 'em all myself, I did!"

The Mole was tremendously interested and excited, and followed the Toad eagerly up the steps and inside. The Rat only snorted and thrust his hands deep into his pockets, remaining where he was.

It was indeed very compact and comfortable. Little sleeping bunks, a little table that folded up against the wall, a cooking stove, lockers, bookshelves, a birdcage with a bird in it, and pots, pans, jugs and kettles of every size and variety.

"All complete!" said the Toad triumphantly, pulling open a locker. "You see – biscuits, potted lobster, sardines – everything you can possibly want. Soda water here, letter paper, bacon, jam, cards and dominoes there. You'll find," he continued, as they descended the steps again, "you'll find that nothing whatever has been forgotten, when we make our start this afternoon."

"I beg your pardon," said the Rat slowly, as he chewed a straw, "but did I overhear you say something about 'we', and 'start', and 'this afternoon'?"

"Now, you dear good old Ratty," said Toad, imploringly, "don't begin talking in that stiff and sniffy sort of way, because you know you really have *got* to come. I can't possibly manage without you, so please consider it settled, and don't argue – it's the one thing I can't stand. You surely don't mean to stick to your dull, fusty old river all your life, and just live in a hole in a bank, and *boat*? I want to show you the world, Ratty! I'm going to make an *animal* of you, my boy!"

"I don't care," said the Rat, doggedly. "I'm not coming, and that's flat. And I *am* going to stick to my old river, *and* live in a hole, *and* boat, as I've always done. And what's more, Mole's going to stick with me and do as I do, aren't you, Mole?"

"Of course I am," said the Mole, loyally. "I'll always stick to you, Rat, and what you say is to be – has got to be. All the same, it sounds as if it might have been – well, rather fun, you know!" he added, wistfully. Poor Mole! The Life Adventurous was so

new a thing to him and so thrilling, and this
fresh aspect of it was so tempting, and he
had fallen in love at first sight with the
canary-coloured cart.

The Rat saw what was passing in his
mind, and wavered. He hated disappointing
people, and he was awfully fond of the
Mole, and would do almost anything to
oblige him. Toad was watching both of
them closely.

"Come along in and have some lunch,"
he said, "and we'll talk it over. We needn't
decide anything in a hurry. Of course, I
don't really care. I only want to give
pleasure to you fellows. 'Live for others!'
That's my motto in life."

Needless to say, after lunch, the old grey

Baffled Beasts and Bamboozled Birds

horse was caught and harnessed. Toad packed the lockers with necessaries, and hung nosebags, onions, bundles of hay, and baskets from the bottom of the cart.

They set off, all talking at once, each animal either trudging by the side of the cart or sitting on the shaft. It was a golden afternoon. The smell of the dust they kicked up was rich and satisfying. Out of orchards on either side of the road, birds called and whistled to them cheerily. Good-natured wayfarers called, "Good-day," or stopped to say nice things about their cart. Rabbits, sitting at their front doors in the hedgerows held up their forepaws and said, "Oh my! Oh my! Oh my!"

They had a pleasant ramble over grassy

downs and along narrow by-lanes, until at last they came out on the high road – and there disaster sprang out on them.

Far behind them they heard a faint warning hum, like the drone of a distant bee. Glancing back, they saw a small cloud of dust, with a dark centre of energy, advancing on them at incredible speed, while from out of the dust a faint 'Poop-poop!' wailed like an uneasy animal in pain. Hardly regarding it, they turned to resume their conversation, when in an instant (as it seemed) the peaceful scene was changed, with a blast of wind and a whirl of sound that made them jump for the nearest ditch.

It was on them! The 'Poop-poop' rang

with a brazen shout in their ears. They had a moment's glimpse of an interior of glittering plate-glass and rich leather. The magnificent motor car – immense, breath-snatching, passionate – with its pilot tense and hugging his wheel, possessed all earth and air for the fraction of a second. Then up flew an enveloping cloud of dust that blinded and enwrapped them utterly, and the car dwindled to a speck in the far distance, changed back into a droning bee once more.

The old grey horse, dreaming, as he plodded along, of his quiet paddock, in a new raw situation such as this simply abandoned himself to his natural emotions. Rearing, plunging, backing steadily, he drove the cart backwards towards the deep ditch at the side of the road. It wavered an instant – then there was a heart-rending *crash* – and the canary-coloured cart, their pride and their joy, lay on its side in the ditch, an irredeemable wreck.

The Rat danced up and down in the road, simply transported with passion. "You villains!" he shouted after it, shaking both fists, "You scoundrels, you highwaymen, you – you – roadhogs! I'll have the law on you! I'll report you! I'll take you through all the courts!"

Meanwhile Toad sat straight down in the middle of the dusty road, his legs stretched out before him, and stared fixedly in the direction of the disappearing motor car. He

breathed short, his face wore a placid
satisfied expression, and at intervals
he murmured, "Poop-poop!"

The Mole was busy
trying to calm the horse,
which he succeeded in doing after a time.
Then he went to look at the cart on its side
in the ditch. It was indeed a sorry sight.

Panels and windows smashed, axles hopelessly bent, one wheel off, sardine tins scattered over the wide world, and the bird in the birdcage sobbing pitifully and calling to be let out.

The Rat came to help him, but their united efforts were not sufficient to right the cart. "Hi! Toad!" they cried. "Come and lend a hand, will you!"

The Toad never answered a word, or budged from his seat in the road, so they went to see what was the matter with him. They found him in a sort of a trance, a happy smile on his face, his eyes still fixed on the dusty wake of their destroyer. At intervals he was still heard to murmur, "Poop-poop!"

The Rat shook him by the shoulder. "Are you coming to help us, Toad?" he demanded sternly.

"Glorious, stirring sight!" murmured Toad, never offering to move. "The poetry of motion! The *real* way to travel! The *only* way to travel! Here today – in next week tomorrow! Villages skipped, towns and cities jumped – always somebody else's horizon! Oh bliss! Oh poop-poop! Oh my! Oh my!"

"Oh *stop* being an ass, Toad!" cried the Mole despairingly.

"And to think I never *knew*!" went on the Toad in a dreamy monotone. "All those wasted years that lie behind me, I never knew, never even *dreamed*! But *now* – but now that I know, now that I fully realize!

Oh what a flowery track lies spread before me, henceforth! What dust clouds shall spring up behind me as I speed on my reckless way! What carts I shall fling carelessly into the ditch in the wake of my magnificent onset! Horrid little carts – common carts – canary-coloured carts!"

"What are we to do with him?" asked the Mole of the Water Rat.

"Nothing at all," replied the Rat firmly. "Because there is really nothing to be done. You see, I know him from of old. He is now possessed. He has got a new craze, and it always takes him that way in its first stage. He'll continue like that for days now, like an animal walking in a happy dream, quite useless for all practical purposes. Never mind him. Let's go and see what there is to be done about the cart."

A careful inspection showed them that, even if they succeeded in righting it by themselves, the cart would travel no longer. The axles were in a hopeless state, and the missing wheel was shattered into pieces.

The Rat knotted the horse's reins over his back and took him by the head, carrying the birdcage and its hysterical occupant in his other hand. "Come on!" he said grimly to the Mole. "It's five or six miles to the nearest town, and we shall just have to walk it. The sooner we make a start the better."

"But what about Toad?" asked the Mole anxiously. "We can't leave him here, in the middle of the road by himself, in the state

he's in! It's not safe. Supposing another Thing were to come along?"

"Oh, *bother* Toad," said the Rat savagely, "I've done with him!"

They had not proceeded very far on their way, however, when there was a pattering of feet behind them. Toad caught them up and thrust a paw inside the elbow of each of them, still breathing short and staring into vacancy.

"Now, look here, Toad!" said the Rat sharply. "As soon as we get to the town, you'll have to go straight to the police station, and see if they know anything about that motor car, and lodge a complaint against it. Then you'll have to arrange for the cart to be fetched and mended. Meanwhile, the Mole and I will go to an inn and find rooms where we can stay till the cart's ready."

"Police station! Complaint!" murmured Toad dreamily. "Me *complain* of that beautiful vision! *Mend the cart!* I've done with carts. I never want to see or to hear of that cart again. Oh, Ratty! You can't think how obliged I am to you for coming on this trip! I wouldn't have gone without you, then I might never have seen that swan, that sunbeam, that thunderbolt! I might never have heard that entrancing sound, or smelled that bewitching smell! I owe it all to you, my best of friends!"

The Rat turned from him in despair. "He's quite hopeless" he said to the Mole. "When we get to the town we'll go to the railway station. With luck we may pick up a train that'll get us back to the riverbank tonight. *Never* let me go a-pleasuring with this provoking animal again!"

The following evening the Mole was sitting on the bank fishing, when the Rat came along to find him. "Heard the news?" he said. "Toad went up to town this morning. He has ordered a large and very expensive motor car."

Why the Bear is Stumpy-Tailed

By Sir George Webbe Dasent

One wintry day, when the fields were covered with snow and ice, and none of the animals could find food, Bruin the Bear met Reynard the Fox. To his surprise, Reynard was slinking along with a string of fish. How Bruin's stomach rumbled! Little did he know that Reynard had stolen them from the home of a farmer down the road. The slow old bear thought that the cunning fox must have come by them himself.

"Where ever did you find those?" asked the Bear, licking his lips.

"Oh my Lord Bruin, I've been out fishing and caught them," said Reynard the Fox.

So Bruin had a mind to learn to fish too. He begged Reynard tell him where to go and how to set about it.

"Oh, it will be an easy craft for you," answered the Fox. "All you've got to do is go out on the lake over the ice, cut a hole and stick your tail down into it. Then go on holding it there as long as you can. Take no notice if your tail smarts a little – that's when the fish bite. Then, when you can wait no longer, pull your tail out as fast and as hard as you can."

Why the Bear is Stumpy-Tailed

Yes, Bruin the Bear did as Reynard the
Fox had said, and held his tail a long, long
time down in the hole, till it was fast
frozen in. Then he pulled it out
with a speedy, strong pull –
and it snapped short off!

And that's why bears go
about with a stumpy tail
this very day.

bran. Then she went home to her mother.

Back again came the rabbit, saying, "Get up! Get up!" and he went up and hit the straw figure on the head, so that it tumbled down.

The rabbit thought that he had killed his bride, and he went away and was very sad.

The Cat and the Mouse

By Joseph Jacobs

T he cat and the mouse played together in the malthouse.

The cat bit the mouse's tail off. "Pray, puss, give me my tail," begged the mouse.

"No," said the cat, "I'll not give you your tail, till you go to the cow and fetch me some milk."

may give cat
milk, that cat may
give me my own tail again."

"Yes," said the baker, "I'll give you
some bread, but if you eat my meal, I'll cut
off your head."

Then the baker gave mouse bread,
and mouse gave butcher bread, and
butcher gave mouse meat, and
mouse gave farmer meat, and
farmer gave mouse hay, and mouse

gave cow hay, and cow gave mouse milk,
and mouse gave cat milk, and cat gave
mouse her own tail again!

The Owl and the Eagle

By Andrew Lang

Once upon a time, in a savage country where the snow lies deep for many months in the year, there lived an owl and an eagle. Though they were so different in many ways they became great friends, and at length set up house together. One hunted during the day and the other, at night. In this manner they did not see very much of each other – but they agreed things were perhaps all the better for that. At any rate they were perfectly happy, and only wanted one thing, or rather, two things, and that was a wife for each.

"I really am too tired when I come home in the evening to clean up the house," said the eagle.

"And I am much too sleepy at dawn after a long night's hunting to begin to sweep and dust," answered the owl.

They both made up their minds that wives they must have.

They flew about in their spare moments to the young ladies of their acquaintance, but the girls all declared they preferred one husband to two. The poor birds began to despair, when, one evening, after they had

been hunting together, they found two
sisters fast asleep in their two beds. The
eagle looked at the owl and the owl looked
at the eagle. "They will make good wives if
they will only stay with us," said they. And
the owl and the eagle flew off to make
themselves look smart before
the girls awoke.

For many hours the sisters
slept on, for they had come a
long way from a town where
there was scarcely
anything to eat, and
felt weak and tired. By
and by they opened their
eyes and saw the two
birds watching them.

"I hope you are rested?" asked the owl politely.

"Oh, yes, thank you," answered the girls. "Only we are so very hungry. Do you think we could have something to eat?"

"Certainly!" replied the eagle, and he flew away to a farmhouse a mile or two off, and brought back a nest of eggs in his strong beak. Meanwhile the owl, catching up a tin pot, went to a cottage where lived an old woman and her cow. Entering the shed by the window the owl dipped the pot into the pail of new milk that stood there.

The girls were so much delighted with the kindness and cleverness of their hosts that, when the birds inquired if they would marry them and stay there forever, they accepted without so much as giving it a second thought. So the eagle took the younger sister as his wife, and the owl the elder, and never was a home more peaceful than theirs!

All went well for several months. Then the eagle's wife had a son, and, on the same day, the owl's wife gave birth to a frog, which she placed directly on the banks of a stream nearby as he did not seem to like the house. The children both grew quickly, and were never tired of playing together, nor wanted any other companions.

One night in the spring, when the ice had melted and the snow was gone, the sisters sat spinning in the house, awaiting their husbands' return. But long though they watched, neither the owl nor the eagle ever came, neither that day nor the next, nor the next, nor the next. At last, being sensible women, they called their children and set out, determined to search the whole world over till their missing husbands were found.

Now the women had no idea in which direction the lost birds had gone, but they knew that some distance off was a thick forest where good hunting was to be found. It seemed a likely place to find them, and they walked quickly on.

Suddenly the younger sister, who was a little in front, gave a cry of surprise.

"Oh! Look at that lake!" she said. "We shall never get across it."

"Yes we shall," answered the elder, "I know what to do." And taking a long piece of string from her pocket, tied one end to a boulder on the bank and fastened the other end into the frog's mouth.

"You must swim across the lake to the other side," she said, stooping to put him in, "and we will walk across on the line behind you." And so they did.

When at last they reached the other side, the owl's wife untied the line from the frog's mouth and told him he could rest and play by the lake till they got back from the forest. Then she and her sister and the boy walked on, until they saw some smoke curling up from a little hut in front of them.

"Let us go in and ask for some water," said the eagle's wife, and in they went.

There, in a dark corner, tied by wings
and feet, and with their eyes sunken, were
their husbands! Quick as lightning, the
wives cut the ties that bound them,
but the poor birds were too
weak from pain and
starvation to do
more than utter soft
sounds of joy.

Then a voice of
thunder made the two
sisters jump, while the
little boy clung tightly
round his mother's neck.
"What are you doing in my house?"
cried the witch – for a witch it was. The
wives answered boldly that they had found

their husbands and were going to save them.

"I shan't let my prisoners go as easily as all that!" she said. "Make my hair grow as thick and as black as yours, or else your husbands shall never see daylight again."

"That is quite simple," replied the elder sister, "only you must do as we did — and perhaps you won't like the treatment."

"If you can bear it, of course I can," answered the witch.

So the girls told her they had first smeared their heads with tar and then laid hot stones upon them. "It is very painful," said they, "but there is no other way that we know of. In order to make sure that all will go right, one of us will hold you down while the other pours on the tar."

And so they did. The elder sister let down her hair till it hung over the witch's eyes, so that she might believe it was her own hair growing. Then the other brought a huge stone – and, in short, that was the end of the witch.

When the sisters saw that she was dead they went to the hut, and nursed their husbands better. Then they picked up the frog, and they all went to make another home on the other side of the lake.

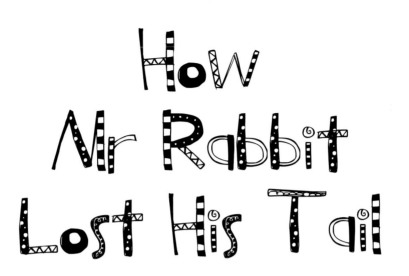

How Mr Rabbit Lost His Tail

By Albert Bigelow Paine

"Once upon a time," said Mr Rabbit at storytime, "a great many great-grandfathers back, my family had long bushy tails like Mr Squirrel and Mr Fox, only a good deal longer and finer and softer, and very handsome."

When Mr Rabbit said that, Mr Squirrel

yards of that rail fence half a mile away, and then beat you across it. Just travel along, and some time this afternoon when you get down that way, I'll come back and let you see me go by. But you'll have to look quick, for I'll be going fast.'

"But Mr Tortoise said he didn't want any start at all, that he was ready to begin the race right then. That made Grandpaw Hare laugh so loud that Mr Fox heard him as he was passing, and came over to see what the fun was. Mr Fox said that he hadn't much to do for a few minutes, and that he'd stay and act as judge. He thought a race like that wouldn't last long – and it didn't, though it wasn't at all the kind of a race he had expected.

"Well, he put Mr Tortoise and my
twenty-seventh great-grandfather side by
side, and then he stood off and said, 'Go!'
He thought it would be over in a minute.

"Grandpaw Hare gave one great big
leap, about twenty feet long,
and then stopped. He
wanted to have some fun
with Mr Tortoise. He
looked around to
where Mr Tortoise
was coming
straddling and
panting along, and
he laughed and rolled
over to see how
solemn he looked,

and how he was travelling as if he meant to get somewhere before dark. Mr Tortoise was down on all fours so he could use all his legs at once, and anybody would think, to look at him, that he really expected to win the race.

"The more my Grandpaw Hare looked at him the more he laughed. Then he would make another long leap forward and stop, and look back, and wait for Mr Tortoise to catch up again.

"Then he would call to him, or maybe go back, and say, 'Come along there, old tobacco box. Are you tied to something?' Mr Fox would laugh a good deal, too, and he told my ancestor to go on and finish the race – that he couldn't wait around there all day. Pretty soon Mr Fox said if they were going to fool along like that, he'd just go down to the fence and take a nap till they got there. He told Grandpaw Hare to call to him when he really started to come, so he could wake up and judge the finish.

"Mr Fox loped away to the fence, and laid down and went to sleep in the shade. Grandpaw Hare thought it would be fun to pretend to be asleep, too. I've heard a story told about it that says that he really did go to sleep, and that Mr Tortoise went by him and got to the fence before he woke up. But that is not the way it happened. My twenty-seventh great-grandfather was too smart to go to sleep, and even if he had gone to sleep, Mr Tortoise made enough noise pawing and scratching along to wake up forty of our family.

"My ancestor would wait until Mr Tortoise came along and was up even with him, then suddenly he'd sit up as if he'd been waked out of a nice dream and say, 'Hello! What do you want to wake me up for when I'm trying to get a nap?' Then he would laugh a big laugh and make another leap, and lie down and pretend again, with his fine plumy tail very handsome in the sun.

"But Grandpaw Hare carried the joke a little too far. He kept letting Mr Tortoise get up a little closer and closer every time, until Mr Tortoise would almost step on him before he would move. And that was just

what Mr Tortoise wanted, for the next time
he came along he came right up behind my
ancestor. Instead of stepping on him,
Mr Tortoise gave his head a quick snap, just
as if he were catching
fish. He grabbed my
Grandpaw Hare by
that beautiful plumy
tail, and held on.
My ancestor gave a
squeal and a holler,
and set out for that
rail fence, telling his
troubles as he came.

"Mr Fox had gone
sound asleep and didn't hear the rumpus at
first. When he did he thought Grandpaw

was just calling to him to wake up and be ready to judge the race, so he sat up quick and watched them come. He saw my twenty-seventh great-grandfather sailing along, with something that looked like an old rusty washpan tied to his tail.

"When Mr Fox saw what it was, he just laid down, and laughed, and rolled over, and then hopped up on the top rail and called out, 'All right, I'm awake, Mr Hare! Come right along, Mr Hare. Come right along! You'll beat him yet!'

"Then Mr Fox saw my ancestor stop and shake himself, and paw, and roll over, to try to get Mr Tortoise loose. This of course he couldn't do, for, as we all know, whenever any of the Turtle family get a grip they never let go till it thunders, and this was a bright day. So pretty soon Grandpaw was up and running again, with Mr Tortoise sailing out behind. Mr Fox laughed to see them coming, and called out, 'Come right along, Mr Hare! Come right along! You'll beat him yet!'

"But Mr Fox made a mistake about that. Grandpaw Hare was really ahead, of course, when he came down the home stretch, but when he got pretty close to the fence he made one more try to get Mr Tortoise loose. He gave himself and his tail a great big swing. But Mr Tortoise didn't let go quite quick enough, and off came my twenty-seventh great-grandfather's beautiful plumy tail, and

covered that much ground in half a day alone. He asked Mr Fox if he was going to let that great straddle bug ruin his reputation for speed and make him the laughing stock of the Big Deep Woods, besides all the other damage he had done.

"Then Mr Fox scratched his head, and thought. He said he didn't see how he could help giving the race to Mr Tortoise, for it was to be the first one across the fence, and Mr Tortoise was certainly the first one across, and he'd gone over the top rail in style.

"Well, that made Grandpaw Hare madder than ever. He didn't say another word, but just picked up his property that Mr Tortoise handed him through the fence, and set out for home by a back way. He was thinking what he ought to do to keep everybody from laughing at him, and he thought that if he didn't do something he'd have to leave the country or drown himself. He had always been so proud that if people laughed at him he knew he could never show his face again.

"And that," said Mr Rabbit, "is the true story of that old race between the hare and the tortoise, and of how the first rabbit came to lose his tail."

The Hare-Brained Crocodiles

An extract from *The White Hare and the Crocodiles*
by Yei Theodora Ozaki

Long, long ago, when all the animals could talk, there lived in the province of Inaba in Japan, a little white hare. His home was on the island of Oki, and just across the sea was the mainland of Inaba.

Now the hare was bored with life on the tiny island of Oki and wanted very much to

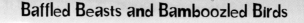

"Oh, no, I am not at all lonely," said the hare, "but as it was such a fine day I came out here to enjoy myself. Won't you stop and play with me a little while?"

The bored crocodile was delighted at the suggestion. He came out of the sea and sat on the shore, and the two played together for some time. Then the hare said, "Mr Crocodile, you live in the sea and I live on this island, and we do not often meet, so I know very little about you. Tell me, do you think the number of your company is greater than mine?"

"Of course, there are more crocodiles than hares," answered the crocodile haughtily. "Can you not see that for yourself? You live on this small

island, while I live in the sea, which spreads
through all parts of the world. If I call
together all the crocodiles who dwell in

"Hmm," said Bruin, "and what was the baby's name this time?"

"Half-eaten," said Reynard.

Bruin thought that a very strange name, but before he had wondered long over it, he began to yawn and gape, and he fell asleep. Well, Bruin hadn't lain long before Reynard the Fox jumped up as he had done twice before, bawled out, "Yes," and ran off to the jar, which this time he finished right off.

When he got back he told Bruin that he had been invited to yet another christening, and when the Bear wanted to know the baby's name, he answered, "All-gone."

After that they laid down again, and slept for a long time. Then they got up to go to the jar to look at the butter. When they found it eaten up, the Bear threw the blame on the Fox, and the Fox on the Bear, and each said the one had been at the jar while the other slept.

"Well, well," said Reynard, "we'll soon find this out, which of us has eaten the butter. We'll just lay down in the sunshine, and he whose cheeks and chaps are greasiest when we wake, he is the thief."

Bruin thought that was fair and sensible,

and as he knew in his heart he had never so much as tasted the butter, he lay down without a care to sleep in the sun.

Then Reynard stole off to the jar for a morsel of butter, which was stuck there in a crack, and then he crept back to the Bear, and greased his chaps and cheeks with it. Then

Reynard, too, lay down to sleep as if nothing had happened.

So when they both woke, the sun had melted the butter, and the Bear's whiskers were all greasy. So it was Bruin after all, and no one else, who had eaten the butter.

How the Leopard Got His Spots

By Rudyard Kipling

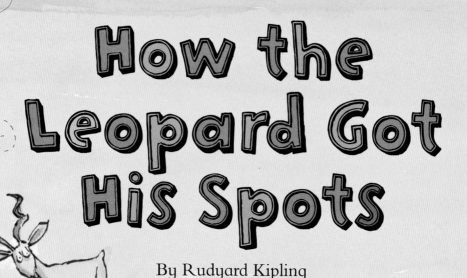

Long, long ago, the Leopard lived in the 'sclusively bare, hot, shiny High Veldt, where there was sand and sandy-coloured rock and 'sclusively tufts of sandy-yellowish grass. The Giraffe and the Zebra and the Eland and the Koodoo and the

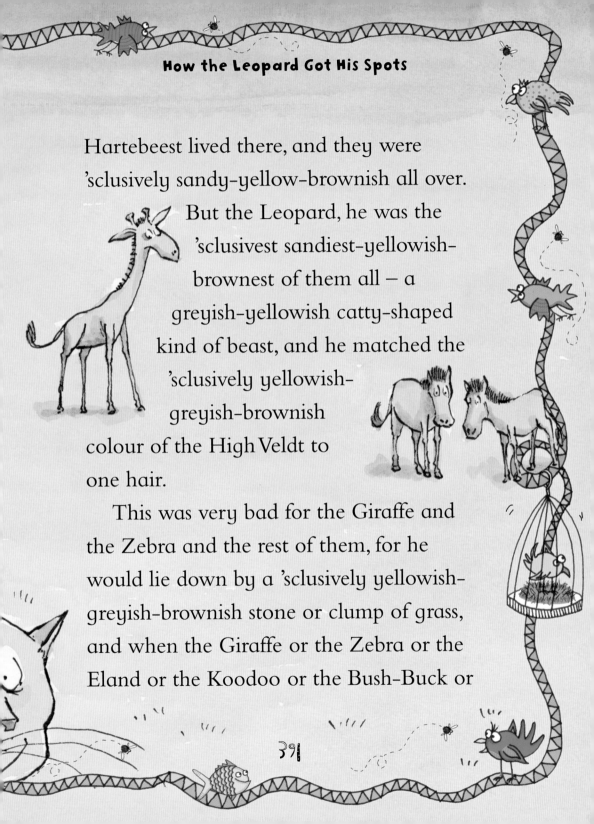

Hartebeest lived there, and they were 'sclusively sandy-yellow-brownish all over. But the Leopard, he was the 'sclusivest sandiest-yellowish-brownest of them all — a greyish-yellowish catty-shaped kind of beast, and he matched the 'sclusively yellowish-greyish-brownish colour of the High Veldt to one hair.

This was very bad for the Giraffe and the Zebra and the rest of them, for he would lie down by a 'sclusively yellowish-greyish-brownish stone or clump of grass, and when the Giraffe or the Zebra or the Eland or the Koodoo or the Bush-Buck or

forest. Meanwhile the Leopard and the
Ethiopian ran about over the 'sclusively
greyish-yellowish-reddish High Veldt
outside, wondering where their breakfasts
and their dinners and their teas had gone.

At last they were so hungry that they ate
rats and beetles and rock-
rabbits, the Leopard
and the Ethiopian,
and then they both had
the big tummy-ache. Then
they met Baviaan – the
dog-headed, barking
Baboon, who is quite
the wisest animal in
All South Africa.

Said Leopard to

Baviaan, "Where has all the game gone?"

Then said Baviaan, "The game has gone into other spots. My advice to you, Leopard, is to go into other spots as soon as you can. And my advice to you, Ethiopian, is to change as soon as you can."

That puzzled the Leopard and the Ethiopian, but they set off to look. Presently, after ever so many days, they saw a great, high, tall forest full of tree trunks all 'sclusively speckled and sprottled and spottled, dotted and splashed and slashed and hatched with shadows.

"What is this," said the Leopard, "that is so 'sclusively dark, and yet so full of little pieces of light?"

"I don't know," said the Ethiopian, "but I

going to sit on your head till morning, because there is something about you that I don't understand."

Presently he heard a grunt and a crash and a scramble, and the Ethiopian called out, "I've caught a thing that I can't see. It smells like Giraffe, and it kicks like Giraffe, but it hasn't any form."

"Don't you trust it," said the Leopard. "Sit on its head till the morning, same as me. They haven't any form – any of 'em."

So they sat down on them hard till bright morning time, and then Leopard said, "What have you at your end of the table, Brother?"

The Ethiopian scratched his head and said, "It ought to be Giraffe, but it is covered

all over with chestnut blotches. What have
you at your end of the table, Brother?"

The Leopard scratched his head and
said, "It ought to be Zebra, but it is covered
all over with black and grey stripes. What
have you been doing to yourself, Zebra?
Don't you know that if you were on the
High Veldt I could see you ten miles off?"

"Yes," said the Zebra,
"but this isn't the
High Veldt.

Can't you see, Leopard?"

"I can now," said the Leopard. "But I couldn't all yesterday. How is it done?"

"Let us up," said the Zebra, "and we will show you."

They let the Zebra and the Giraffe get up. The Zebra moved away to some little thorn bushes where the sunlight fell all stripy, and Giraffe moved off to some tallish trees where the shadows fell all blotchy.

"Now watch," said the Zebra and the Giraffe. "This is the way it's done. One – two – three! And where's your breakfast?"

Leopard stared, and Ethiopian stared, but all they could see were stripy and blotched shadows in the forest, but no a sign of Zebra and Giraffe. They had just walked off and hidden themselves in the shadowy forest.

"Hi! Hi!" said the Ethiopian. "That's a trick worth learning. Take a lesson by it, Leopard. You show up in this dark place like a bar of soap in a coal bucket."

"Ho! Ho!" said the Leopard. "Would it surprise you very much to know that you show up in this dark place like a mustard plaster on a sack of coals?"

"Well, calling names won't catch dinner," said the Ethiopian. "The long and the little of it is that we don't match our backgrounds. Baviaan's told me I ought to change, and as I've nothing to change except my skin, I'm going to change that."

"What to?" said the Leopard, tremendously excited.

"To a nice working blackish-brownish colour, with a little purple in it, and touches of slaty-blue. It will be the very thing for hiding in hollows and behind trees."

He changed his skin then and there, and the Leopard was more excited than ever – he had never seen a man change his skin.

"But what about me?" he said, when the Ethiopian had worked his last little finger into his fine new black skin.

"You take Baviaan's advice too. He told you to go into spots. I'll make 'em with the tips of my fingers," said the Ethiopian. "There's plenty of black left on my skin."

"All right," said the Leopard, "but don't make 'em too vulgar-big. I wouldn't want to look like Giraffe – not forever so."

Then the Ethiopian put his five fingers close together and pressed them all over the Leopard. Wherever the five fingers touched they left five little black marks, all close together. Sometimes the fingers slipped and the marks got a little blurred, but if you look closely at any Leopard now you will see that there are always five spots – off five black fingertips.

"Now you are a beauty!" said the Ethiopian. "You can lie out on the bare ground and look like a heap of pebbles. You can lie out on the rocks and look like a piece of pudding stone. You can lie out on a leafy branch and look like sunshine sifting through the leaves, and you can lie right across a path and look like nothing in

particular. Think of that and
purr! Now come along, we'll
see if we can't get even with Mr One-
Two-Three Where's your Breakfast!"
So they went away and lived happily
ever afterward. That is all.

404

The Three Goslings

An Italian fairy tale
retold by Thomas Frederick Crane

Once upon a time there were three goslings who were afraid of the wolf, for if he found them he would eat them. One day the largest gosling said, "I think we had better build a little house to protect us from the wolf. Let's go and look for something to build it with."

So they went and found a man who had a load of straw, and he gave them as much

"No, I am still busy and I don't want anyone in the way," replied the gosling. "But you can try a bit of macaroni to see if it is well cooked. Put your mouth to the hole in the wall and I will poke it through."

So the wolf, all greedy, put his mouth to the hole. Then the gosling took the kettle of boiling water and poured it, instead of the macaroni, through the hole into the wolf's mouth. The wolf was scalded and killed.

Then the gosling took a knife and cut open the wolf's stomach. Out jumped the other two goslings, who were still alive, for the wolf was so greedy that he had swallowed them whole. Then these goslings begged their sister's pardon for the mean way in which they had treated her, and she, because she was kind-hearted, forgave them and took them into her house.

There they ate their macaroni and lived together, happy and contented.

Scarily Stupid, Dangerously Dumb

The Fish and the Hare

By Andrew Lang

Once upon a time an old man and his wife lived together in a little village. One day, the old man was walking in a forest nearby when his foot sank into some soft, newly turned earth. Curious, he dug and dug, and at last he uncovered a pot full of gold and silver.

'Oh, what luck!' he thought. 'But I can't

take it home because my wife is a terrible
gossip – once she knows, she'll tell the
whole world!'

He thought hard and made a plan. He
covered up the pot again with earth and
went to market, where he bought a live pike
and a live hare. Then he hurried back to
the forest and hung the pike up at the top
of a tree and tied up the hare at the edge of
a stream. Then he trotted merrily home.

"Wife!" he cried. "I've found a pot full of
treasure in the forest! Come with me and
we'll fetch it."

So the man and his excited wife drove to
the forest.

On the way, the man said, "What
strange things one hears, wife! I was told

only the other day that fish now live in the treetops and some wild animals spend their time in the water. Well, well! Times are certainly changed."

"You must be crazy, husband!" replied she. "Dear, what nonsense people do talk."

Of course, it wasn't long before the couple came across the pike flapping at the top of the tree and the hare wriggling in the water — and the wife was flabbergasted. Lost for words, the man drove his wife to where the treasure was buried, and they dug up the pot and drove home again.

So now the old couple had plenty of money. But the wife was very foolish, and every day she asked lots of people to dinner and laid on huge feasts for them. Her husband grew cross that she was spending away their fortune.

The woman just went straight off to the governor to complain.

"Oh, my lord!" she moaned. "Ever since my husband found the treasure there is no bearing him. He only eats and drinks, and won't work, and he keeps all the money to himself."

The governor took pity on the woman, and ordered his secretary to go to the man's house and take the treasure for safekeeping.

But the old man just shrugged his shoulders and said, "What treasure? I know nothing about treasure. Pardon me, Your Excellency, but my wife must have dreamed of it. She is not in her right mind, sir. Ask

her how it all happened."

"Well, Mr Secretary," cried the wife, "we were driving through the forest, and we saw a pike at home in the top of a tree and a hare living in the stream—"

"What rubbish! Are you making fun of me?" shouted the secretary, losing his temper. And he turned on his heel and drove back to the town.

After that the old woman had to hold her tongue, and the man spent part of the treasure in opening a shop. He prospered and spent the rest of his days in peace.

Buttercup

By George Webbe Dasent

Once upon a time there was an old wife
who sat and baked. Now, you must know
that this old wife had a little son, who was
so plump and fat and so fond of good
things, that they called him Buttercup. She
had a dog, too, whose name was Goldtooth.
One day, as she was baking, all at once
Goldtooth began to bark.

"Run out, Buttercup, there's a dear," said

the old wife, "and see what Goldtooth is barking at."

So the boy ran out, and came back crying out, "Oh, heaven help us! Here comes a great big, ugly, old witch with a bag on her back."

"Jump under the table and hide yourself," said his mother.

Then in came the old hag. "Good day," said she.

"God bless you!" said Buttercup's mother.

"Isn't your Buttercup at home today?" asked the hag.

"No, that he isn't. He's out in the wood with his father, shooting grouse."

"Plague take it," said the hag, "for I had a little silver knife I wanted to give him."

"Pip, pip! Here I am," said Buttercup from under the table, and out he came.

"I'm so old and stiff in the back," said the hag, "you must creep into the bag and fetch it out for yourself."

So Buttercup opened the bag and crept inside it. But as soon as he was well inside, the hag threw the bag over her back and strode off.

When they had gone a good bit of the way, the old hag got tired and asked, "How far is it to Snoring?"

"Half a mile," answered Buttercup.

So the hag put the sack down on the road, and went by herself into the wood and lay down to sleep. Meanwhile, Buttercup set to work and cut a hole in the sack with his knife. Then he crept out and put the great root of a fir tree into the sack, and ran home to his mother. When the hag got home and discovered what was in the sack, she was in a fine rage.

Next day the old wife sat and baked again, and her dog began to bark, just as he did the day before. "Run out, Buttercup, my boy," said she, "and see what Goldtooth is barking at."

"Well, I never!" cried Buttercup as soon as he looked outside. "If it isn't that ugly old beast coming again with a great sack on her back."

"Under the table with you and hide," said his mother.

"Good day!" said the hag. "Is your Buttercup at home today?"

"I'm sorry to say he isn't," said his mother, "he's out in the wood with his father, shooting grouse."

"What a bore!" said the hag, "here I have a beautiful little silver spoon I want to give him."

"Pip, pip! Here I am," said Buttercup, and he crept out.

"I'm so stiff in the back," said the old witch, "you must creep into the sack and fetch it out for yourself."

So when Buttercup was well into the
sack, the hag swung it over her shoulders
and set off home as fast as her legs could
carry her. But when they had gone a good
bit she grew weary, and asked, "How far is
it to Snoring?"

"A mile and a half," answered Buttercup.

So the hag set down the sack, and went
into the wood to sleep a bit. While she slept,
Buttercup made a hole in the sack and got
out, and put a great stone into it instead.

When the old witch got home she made
a great fire and put a big pot on it, and got
everything ready to boil up Buttercup. But
when she took the sack and thought she
was going to turn out Buttercup into the
pot, down plumped the stone and made a

But when Buttercup was well inside the sack the old hag swung it across her shoulders, and set off as fast as she could. This time she did not stop to sleep on the way, but went straight home with Buttercup in the sack.

It was Sunday, so the old hag said to her daughter, "Now you must take Buttercup and cook him up nicely till I come back, for I'm off to church to ask my guests to come for dinner."

So, when all in the house had gone to church, the daughter was to kill Buttercup, but she didn't know how to set about it.

"Stop a bit," said Buttercup, "I'll show you how to do it. Just lay your head on the chopping block, and you'll soon see."

So the poor silly thing laid her head
down, and Buttercup took an axe and
chopped off her head,
just as if she had been
a chicken.

Then Buttercup took all the gold and
silver that lay in the old hag's house, and
went home to his mother, and became a
rich man.

The Darning Needle

By Hans Christian Andersen

There was once a Darning Needle who thought herself so fine, she imagined she was an embroidering needle. "Take care, and mind you hold me tight!" she said to the Fingers that took her out. "Don't let me fall! If I fall on the ground I shall certainly never be found again, for I am so fine!"

"That's as it may be," said the Fingers, and they grasped her round the body.

"See, I'm coming with a train!" said the Darning Needle, and she drew a long thread after her.

The Fingers pointed the needle just at the cook's slipper, in which the leather had burst and was to be sewn together.

"That's common work," said the Darning Needle. "I shall never get through. I'm far too fine. I'm breaking! I'm breaking!" And she really broke. "Did I not say so?" said the Darning Needle.

"Now this needle's quite useless," said the Fingers, but they were obliged to hold her all the same, for the cook dropped some sealing wax upon the needle to stick her back together again, and pinned the ends of her neck scarf together with it in front.

"So, now I'm a brooch!" said the Darning Needle. "I knew very well that I should become important!" And she laughed quietly to herself – of course one can never see when a Darning Needle laughs. There she sat, as proud as if she were in a state coach, and looked all about her. In fact, the Darning Needle drew herself up so proudly that she fell out of the neck scarf right into the sink, which the cook was rinsing out.

"Now I'm going on a journey," said the Darning Needle. "If I only don't get lost!"

But of course, she washed down the pipe and out into the drain and really was lost.

"I'm too fine for this world," she observed, as she lay in the gutter. "But I know who I am, and there's always something in that!"

So the Darning Needle kept her proud behaviour, and did not lose her good humour. Things of many kinds swam over her — chips and straws and pieces of old newspapers.

"Only look how they sail!" said the Darning Needle. "They don't know what is under them! I'm here, I remain firmly here. See, there goes a chip thinking of nothing in the world but of himself – of a chip! There's a straw going by now. How he turns! How he twirls about! Don't think only of yourself, you might easily run up against a stone. There swims a bit of newspaper. What's written upon it has long been forgotten, and yet it gives itself airs. I sit quietly and patiently here. I know who I am, and I shall remain what I am."

One day something lay close beside her that glittered splendidly. The Darning Needle believed that it was a diamond, but it was a bit of broken bottle, and because it shone, the Darning Needle spoke to it, introducing herself as a brooch. "I suppose you are a diamond?" she observed.

"Why, yes, something of that kind."

Each believed the other to be a very valuable thing, and they began speaking about the world and how important they were in it.

"And now we sit here and glitter!" said the Bit of Bottle. But at that very moment more water came into the gutter and the Bit of Bottle was carried away.

"So he has gone," observed the Darning Needle. "I remain here. I am too fine." And proudly she sat there, and had many great thoughts. "I could almost believe I had been born of a sunbeam, I'm so fine! It really appears as if the sunbeams were always seeking for me under the water."

One day a couple of boys were playing in the gutter, where they sometimes found old nails, pennies and similar treasures. It was dirty work, but they took delight in it.

"Oh!" cried one, who had pricked himself with the Darning Needle. "There's a fellow for you!"

"I'm not a fellow, I'm a young lady!" said the Darning Needle.

But nobody listened to her. The sealing wax had come off and she had turned black, but black makes one look slender, and she thought herself finer than ever.

"Here comes an eggshell sailing along!" said the boys, and they stuck the Darning

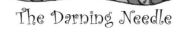

Needle fast in the eggshell.

"White walls, and black myself! That looks well," remarked the Darning Needle. "Now one can see me. I only hope I shall not be seasick!" But she was not seasick at all. "The finer one is, the more one can bear," she remarked.

Crack! went the eggshell, as a bicycle rode over her.

"Good heavens, how it crushes one!" said the Darning Needle. "I'm getting seasick now – I'm quite sick."

But she was not really sick, though the bicycle went over her – she lay there at full length, and there she may still lie.

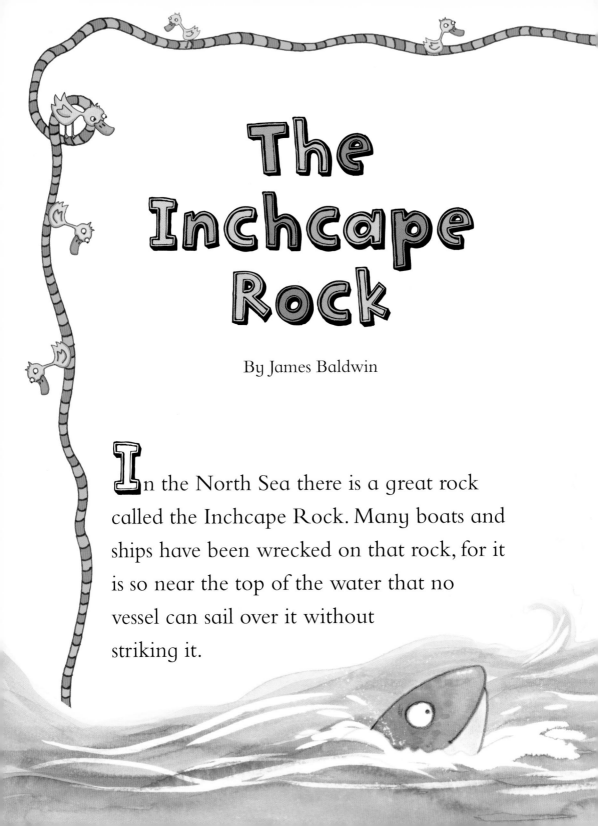

The Inchcape Rock

By James Baldwin

In the North Sea there is a great rock called the Inchcape Rock. Many boats and ships have been wrecked on that rock, for it is so near the top of the water that no vessel can sail over it without striking it.

More than a hundred years ago there lived not far away a kind-hearted man who was called the Abbot of Aberbrothock. "It is a pity," he said, "that so many sailors should lose their lives on that rock."

So the abbot got a buoy fastened to the rock with a strong chain. It floated back and forth in the shallow water. On the top of the buoy was a bell, and when the waves dashed against it,

the bell would ring out loud and clear.

Now, sailors were no longer afraid to cross the sea at that place. When they heard the bell ringing, they knew just where the rock was, and they steered their vessels around it. "God bless the good Abbot of Aberbrothock!" they all said.

One calm summer day, a ship with a black flag happened to sail not far from the Inchcape Rock. The ship belonged to a sea robber called Ralph the Rover. He was a terror to all honest people on sea and shore.

There was little wind that day, and the sea was as smooth as glass. The ship stood almost still – there was hardly a breath of air to fill her sails.

Ralph the Rover was walking on the

deck. He looked out upon the sea, and saw the buoy floating above the Inchcape Rock. But the bell was not ringing – there were no waves to set it in motion.

"Boys!" cried Ralph the Rover. "Put out the boat and row me to the Inchcape Rock. We will play a trick on the old abbot."

The boat was lowered. Strong arms soon rowed it to the Inchcape Rock. Then the robber, with a heavy axe, broke the chain that held the buoy. He cut the fastenings of the bell and it fell into the water. There was a gurgling sound as it sank out of sight.

"The next one that comes this way will not bless the abbot," said Ralph the Rover.

Soon a breeze sprang up and the black ship sailed away. The sea robber laughed as

he looked back and saw that there was
nothing to mark the place of the rock.

For many days, Ralph the Rover scoured
the seas, and plundered many ships. At last
he chanced to sail back toward the place
from which he had started.

The wind had blown hard all day. The
waves rolled high. The ship was moving
swiftly. But in the evening the wind died
away, and a thick fog came on.

Ralph the Rover walked the deck. He
could not see where the ship was going. "If
the fog would only clear away!" he said.

"I thought I heard the roar of breakers,"
said the pilot. "We must be near the shore."

"I cannot tell," said Ralph the Rover,
"but I think we are not far from the

Inchcape Rock. I wish we could hear the good abbot's bell."

The next moment there was a great crash. "It is the Inchcape Rock!" the sailors cried, as the ship gave a lurch to one side, and began to sink.

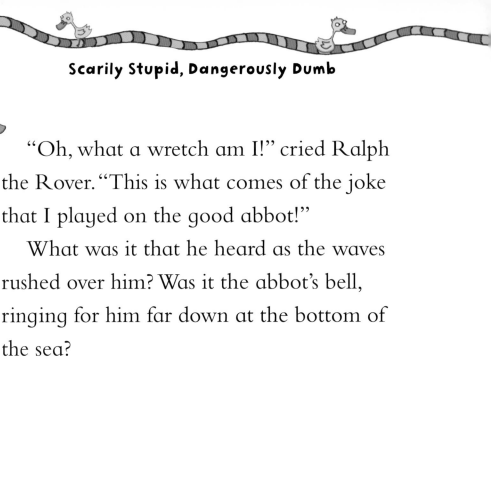

"Oh, what a wretch am I!" cried Ralph the Rover. "This is what comes of the joke that I played on the good abbot!"

What was it that he heard as the waves rushed over him? Was it the abbot's bell, ringing for him far down at the bottom of the sea?

The Foolish Weaver

By Andrew Lang

⊙nce there was a weaver who was in want of work, and he took service with a farmer as a shepherd. The farmer knew that the man was very slow-witted and gave him very careful instructions as to everything that he was to do. He ended up by saying, "If a wolf or any wild animal tries to hurt the flock, you should pick up a big stone like this" – and he demonstrated –

"and throw a few at him. He will be afraid and run away." The weaver said that he understood, and set off, taking the sheep to the hills to graze.

By chance in the afternoon a leopard appeared, so the weaver instantly ran home as fast as he could to get the stones which the farmer had shown him, to throw at the creature. When he came back all the flock were scattered or killed!

When the farmer heard the tale he gave the weaver a sound scolding. "Were there no stones

on the hillside?" he cried. "You didn't have to run back here and get these exact ones, you fool! You are not fit to herd sheep. Today you shall stay at home and mind my old mother who is sick – perhaps you will be able to drive flies off her face, if you can't drive beasts away from sheep!"

So, the weaver was left at home to take care of the farmer's old, sick mother. Now as she lay outside on a bed, it turned out that the flies became very troublesome. The weaver looked round for something to drive them away with, and as he had been told to pick up the nearest stone to drive the beasts away from the flock, he thought he would this time show how cleverly he could obey orders. Accordingly, he seized the nearest

stone, which was a big, heavy one, and
tossed it at the flies. Of course, very
unhappily, he killed the poor old woman
also! Then, being afraid of the wrath of the
farmer, he fled and was not seen again in
that neighbourhood.

All that day and all the next night he
walked, and at length he came to a village
where a great many weavers lived
together.

"You are welcome," said
they. "Eat and sleep, for
tomorrow six of us start
in search of fresh wool
to weave, and we
pray you to give us
your company."

The Foolish Weaver

"Willingly," answered the weaver. So the next morning the seven weavers set out to go to the village where they could buy what they wanted. On the way they had to cross a ravine, which lately had been full of water, but now was quite dry. However, the weavers were accustomed to swimming over this ravine. Regardless of the fact that it was dry, they stripped and, tying their clothes on their heads, started to swim across the dry sand and rocks that formed the bed of the ravine.

The weavers got to the other side without further damage than bruised knees and elbows, and as soon as they were over, one of them began to count everybody to make sure that all were safely there. He counted all except himself, and then cried out that somebody was missing! This set each of them counting, but each made the same mistake of counting all except himself, so that they became certain that one of them was missing! They ran up and down the bank of the ravine, wringing their hands in great distress and looking for signs of their lost comrade.

Then a farmer found them and asked what was the matter. "Alas!" said one. "Seven of us started from the other bank

and one must have been drowned on the crossing, as we can only find six remaining!"

The farmer eyed them a minute. Then, picking up his stick, he dealt each a sounding blow, counting as he did so, "One! Two! Three!" and so on up to seven.

When the weavers found that there were seven of them they were full of gratitude for the man whom they thought must be a magician – for he could make seven out of what was obviously just six people.

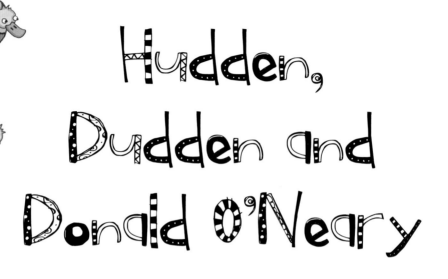

Hudden, Dudden and Donald O'Neary

By Joseph Jacobs

Once upon a time there were two
farmers, and their names were Hudden and
Dudden. They had poultry in their yards,
sheep on the uplands, and scores of cattle in
the meadow alongside the river. But for all
that they weren't happy, for just between
their two farms there lived a poor man by

the name of Donald O'Neary. He had just
a hovel to live in and a strip of grass next to
it that was barely enough to keep his one
cow, Daisy, from starving. You would think
there was little here to make Hudden and
Dudden jealous, but so it is that the more
one has, the more one wants. Donald's
neighbours would lie awake at night,
scheming how they might get hold of his
little strip of grass.

One day Hudden said to Dudden, "Let's
kill Daisy – if that doesn't make him clear
out, nothing will."

No sooner said than agreed. It wasn't
dark before Hudden and Dudden crept up
to the little shed where Daisy lay, trying her
best to chew the cud, though she hadn't had

as much grass in the day as would cover your hand. Later on, when Donald came to see if Daisy was all snug for the night, the poor beast had only time to lick his hand once before she died.

Downhearted though Donald was, he began to wonder if he could get any good out of Daisy's death. The next day he trudged off to the fair, with Daisy's hide over his shoulder and every penny he had jingling in his pockets. Just before he got to the fair, he made several slits in the hide and put a penny in each one. Then he walked into the best inn of the town and, hanging the hide up to a nail in the wall, sat down.

"Some of your best whisky," said Donald to the landlord. But the landlord didn't like

his looks. "Are you afraid I won't pay you?" asked Donald. "Why, I have a hide here that gives me all the money I want." And with that he gave the hide a good whack with his stick, and out dropped a penny.

The landlord's eyes opened wide, and he said, "What'll you take for that hide?"

"It's not for sale, my good man," said Donald.

"Will you take a gold piece for it?" asked the landlord

"It's not for sale, I tell you." And with that Donald gave the hide another whack, and out jumped a second penny.

The long and the short of it was that Donald sold the hide to the landlord for thirty gold pieces. Then, that evening, Donald walked up to Hudden's door.

"Good evening, Hudden," said Donald. "Will you lend me your best pair of scales?"

Hudden stared and scratched his head, but he lent the scales to Donald.

When Donald got home, he pulled out his pocketful of gold and began to weigh each piece. But Hudden had put a lump of butter at the bottom of the scales, and so the last piece of gold stuck fast when Donald took them back to Hudden.

As soon as Donald's back was turned, Hudden was off to Dudden's.

"Good evening, Dudden. That vagabond, bad luck to him—"

"You mean Donald O'Neary?"

"Who else should I mean? He's back here weighing sacks of gold."

"How do you know that?" asked Dudden.

"Here are my scales he borrowed, and here's a gold piece still sticking to them," said Hudden, pleased.

457

Off they went together, and they came to Donald's door. Donald had finished making the last pile of ten gold pieces, but he couldn't finish because a piece had stuck to the scales.

In walked Hudden and Dudden without an 'If you please' or 'By your leave'.

"Well, I never!" was all they could manage to say.

"Good evening, Hudden. Good evening, Dudden. Ah! You did me a good turn by killing poor Daisy. When I found her dead, I thought to myself, 'Well, her hide may fetch something,' and it did. Hides are worth their weight in gold in the market just now."

Hudden nudged Dudden, and Dudden winked at Hudden.

"Good evening, Donald O'Neary," and Hudden and Dudden went away.

The next day there wasn't a cow or a calf that belonged to Hudden or Dudden, for all their hides were going to the fair in Hudden's biggest cart, drawn by Dudden's strongest pair of horses.

When they arrived to the fair, each farmer took a hide over his arm, and they walked through the fair shouting out at the tops of their voices, "Hides to sell! Hides to sell."

Out came the tanner and said, "How much for your hides, my good men?"

"Their weight in gold."

"It's early in the day to be drunk!" said the tanner, and back he went to his yard.

"Hides to sell! Fine fresh hides to sell!" cried Hudden and Dudden.

Out came the cobbler and said, "How much for your hides, my good men?"

"Their weight in gold."

"Are you making fun of me?" cried the cobbler. "Take that for your pains!" and he dealt Hudden a whack that made him stagger.

People came running from the other end of the fair. "What's the matter?" they cried.

"Here are a couple of vagabonds selling hides for their weight in gold," said the cobbler.

"Hold 'em fast!" shouted the innkeeper, who was the last to get there. "I'll bet it's one of those two rogues who tricked me out of thirty gold pieces yesterday for a wretched hide."

It was more kicks than halfpence that Hudden and Dudden got before they were on their way home again. If they loved Donald little before, they loved him even less now.

"What's the matter, friends?" said Donald as he saw them hurrying along, their hats knocked in, their coats torn off and their faces black and blue. "Have you been fighting?"

"It's your fault!" they snarled. "You've been lying to us!"

"Who lied to you? Didn't you see the gold with your own eyes?"

But it was no use talking. There was a

sack handy, and into it Hudden and Dudden bundled Donald O'Neary. They tied him up tight, ran a pole through the knot, and off they started on their way for the Brown Lake of the Bog, each with a pole end on his shoulder, and Donald O'Neary between.

But the Brown Lake was far, the road was dusty, and Hudden and Dudden were sore, weary and parched with thirst. There was an inn by the roadside.

"Let's go in," said Hudden. "I'm deadbeat. He's heavy and we've had little to eat."

If Hudden was willing, so was Dudden. As for Donald, he was dumped down outside the inn door for all the world as if

he had been a sack
of potatoes.

"Sit still, you
vagabond," said
Dudden. "If we don't
mind waiting, you
needn't."

Donald held his peace,
but after a while he heard the glasses
clink, and Hudden singing away at the top
of his voice.

"I won't have her I tell you, I won't have
her!" cried Donald, as loud as he could from
inside the sack.

"And who won't you have, may I be so
bold as to ask?" said a farmer, who had just
come up with a drove of cattle, and was

turning in for a drink at the inn.

"It's the King's daughter. They are bothering the life out of me to marry her."

"You're the lucky fellow. I'd give something to be in your shoes."

"Do you see that, now! Wouldn't it be a fine thing for a farmer to be marrying a princess, all dressed in gold and jewels?"

"Jewels, you say? Ah, now, couldn't you take me with you?"

"Well, you are an honest fellow. As I don't care for the King's daughter, though she's as beautiful as the day, and is covered with jewels from top to toe, you shall have her. Just undo the cord and let me out. They tied me up tight as they knew I'd run away from her."

Out crawled Donald from the sack, and in crept the farmer.

"Now lie still, and don't mind the shaking. It's only rumbling over the palace steps. Ah, it's a deal I'm giving up for you, sure as it is that I don't care for the Princess."

"Take my cattle in exchange," said the farmer. And it wasn't long before Donald was at their tails, driving them homeward.

Out came Hudden and Dudden, and the one took one end of the pole, and the other the other.

"I'm thinking he's heavier," said Hudden.

"Ah, never mind," said Dudden, "it's only a step now to the Brown Lake."

"I'll have her now!" shouted out the

farmer from inside the sack.

"By my faith and you shall," said Hudden, and he whacked his stick across the sack.

"I'll have her!" yelled the farmer, louder than ever.

"Here you are," said Dudden, as they reached the Brown Lake. Then, unslinging the sack, they threw it into the lake.

"You'll not be playing your tricks on us any longer," said Hudden.

"True for you," said Dudden. "Ah, Donald, my boy, it was an ill day when you borrowed my scales!"

Off they went,

with a light step and an easy heart, but
when they were near home, whom should
they see but Donald O'Neary? All around
him cows were grazing and calves were
kicking up their heels and butting their
heads together.

"Is it you, Donald?" said Dudden.
"Faith, you've been quicker than us."

"Yes, Dudden, and let me thank
you kindly. The turn was good, even

if the will was ill. You'll have heard, like me, that the Brown Lake leads to the Land of Promise. I always thought it was lies, but it is as true as my word. Look at the cattle."

Hudden stared and Dudden gaped, but they couldn't get over the cattle, and fine, fat cattle they were, too.

"It's only the worst I could bring up with me," said Donald O'Neary, "the others were so fat, there was no driving them. It's a wonder they were happy to leave, with grass as far as you could see, and as sweet and juicy as fresh butter."

"Ah now, Donald, we haven't always been friends," said Dudden, "but, as I was just saying, you were ever a decent lad. You'll show us the way there, won't you?"

"I don't see that I should do that, there is a lot more cattle down there. Why shouldn't I have them all to myself?"

"Faith, they may well say, 'the richer you get, the harder the heart'. You always were a neighbourly lad, Donald. You wouldn't wish to keep the luck all to yourself?"

"True for you, Hudden, though it's a bad example you set me. But I'll not be thinking of old times. There is plenty for all there, so come along with me."

Off they trudged with an eager step. When they came to the Brown Lake the sky was full of clouds, and, if the sky was full, the lake was as full.

"Ah, look! There they are!" cried Donald, and he pointed to the clouds in the lake.

"Where? Where?" cried Hudden.

"Don't be greedy!" cried Dudden, and he jumped his hardest into the lake to be the first to get to the fat cattle. But if he jumped first, Hudden wasn't long behind.

Of course, they never came back. Maybe they got too fat like the cattle. As for Donald O'Neary, he had cattle and sheep all his days to his heart's content.

Mother Hulda

By the Brothers Grimm

A widow had two daughters – one was pretty and hard-working, the other was ugly and lazy. The pretty, hard-working girl was her step-daughter, so the woman made her do all the housework. Every day the poor girl had to sit by a well on the high road and spin until her fingers bled.

Now it happened once that as the spindle was bloody, she dipped it into the

well to wash it, but it slipped out of her hand and fell in. Then she began to cry, and ran to her step-mother to tell her of her misfortune. Her step-mother scolded her, and said in her rage, "As you have let the spindle fall in, you must go and fetch it out again!"

So the girl went back again to the well, not knowing what to do, and in the despair of her heart she jumped down into the well the same way the spindle had gone.

After that she knew nothing. When she came to she was in a

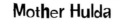

beautiful meadow, and the sun was shining on the flowers that grew around her.

The girl walked on through the meadow until she came to a baker's oven that was full of bread, and the bread called out to her, "Oh, take me out, take me out, or I shall burn. I am baked enough already!" Then she drew near, and with the baker's shovel she took out all the loaves one after the other.

Then she went farther on till she came to a tree weighed down with apples, and it called out to her, "Oh, shake me, shake me, all of my apples are ripe!" The girl shook the tree until the apples fell like rain, and she shook until there were no more to fall, and when she had gathered them together in a heap she went on farther.

At last she came to a little house. An old woman was peeping out of it, but she had such great teeth that the girl was terrified. She was about to run away, when the old woman called her back. "What are you afraid of, my dear child? Come and live with me, and if you do the housework well and keep things orderly, things shall go well for you. You must take great pains to make my bed well, and shake it up thoroughly, so that the feathers fly about – and then in the world it snows, for I am Mother Hulda."

As the old woman spoke so kindly, the girl took courage, consented, and went to her work. She did everything to the old woman's satisfaction, and shook the bed with such a will that the feathers flew about like snowflakes. And so she led a good life, and never had a cross word, but boiled and roasted meat every day.

When she had lived a long time with Mother Hulda, she began to feel sad, but she didn't know why. At last she began to think she must be homesick. Although she was a thousand times better off where she was than at home, still she had a great longing to go back. At last she said to her mistress, "I am homesick, and although I am very well off here, I cannot stay any longer. I must go back to my own home."

Mother Hulda answered, "It pleases me that you should wish to go home, and, as you have served me faithfully, I will send you there!" Mother Hulda took the girl by the hand and led her to a large door. As she stood in the doorway there fell upon her a heavy shower of gold, and the gold hung all about her so that she was covered with it. "All this is yours, because you have worked so hard," said Mother Hulda, and besides that, she gave the spindle back to the girl — the very same spindle that she had dropped in the well.

When she went through the door and it shut behind her, the girl found herself back in the world again, not far from her stepmother's house. As she walked through the yard, the cockerel stood on the top of the well and cried, "Cock-a-doodle doo! Our golden girl has come home too!"

Then the girl went in to her step-mother, and as she had returned covered with gold she was well received.

So the girl told her step-mother what had happened to her, and when the step-mother heard how she came to have such great riches she began to wish that her ugly and lazy daughter might have the same good fortune. So she sent her other daughter to sit by the well and spin, and in order to make her spindle bloody she put her hand into the thorn hedge. Then the lazy daughter threw the spindle into the well, and jumped in herself.

She found herself, like her sister, in the beautiful meadow, and followed the same path. When she came to the baker's oven, the bread cried out, "Oh, take me out, take me out, or I shall burn. I am quite done already!"

But the lazy girl answered, "I have no desire to black my hands," and she went on farther.

Soon she came to the apple tree, which called out, "Oh, shake me, shake me, all of my apples are ripe!"

But the girl answered, "That is all very fine, but suppose one of you should fall on my head," and she went on farther.

When the lazy girl came to Mother Hulda's house she did not feel afraid, as she knew beforehand of her great teeth, and began to work for her at once.

Scarily Stupid, Dangerously Dumb

The first day the girl went to work, she did everything Mother Hulda told her because of the gold she expected. But the second day she began to be lazy, and the third day still more so, so that she would not even get up in the morning. Neither did she make Mother Hulda's bed right, and did not shake it so that the feathers flew about.

Mother Hulda soon grew tired of her, and gave her a warning. The lazy thing was pleased, and thought that now the shower of gold was coming. Mother Hulda led her to the door, but as she stood in the doorway, instead of the shower of gold, a great kettle full of tar was emptied over her. "That is the reward for your service," said Mother Hulda, and shut the door.

So the lazy girl came home all covered with tar, and the cockerel on the top of the well, seeing her, cried, "Cock-a-doodle doo! Our dirty girl has come home too!"

And the tar remained sticking to her fast, and never, as long as she lived, could she get it off.

Which was the Foolishest?

By Andrew Lang

In a little village that stood on a wide plain, where you could see the sun from the moment he rose to the moment he set, there lived two couples side by side. The men, who both worked under the same master, were good friends, but the wives were always quarrelling, and the subject they quarrelled most about was which of the two had the stupidest husband. Each woman thought her own husband the more foolish of the two.

"You should just see what he does!" one woman said to her neighbour. "When he dresses the baby, he puts her frock on upside down, and, one day, I found him trying to feed her with boiling hot soup. Then he picks up stones in the road and sows them instead of potatoes, and one day he wanted to go into the garden from the top window, because he declared it was a shorter way than through the door."

"That is bad enough, of course," answered the other, "but it is really nothing to what I have to endure every day from my husband. If, when I am busy, I ask him to go and feed the hens, he is certain to give them some poisonous stuff instead of their proper food, and when I visit the yard next I find them all dead. Once, when I had gone away to my sick mother, he even took my best bonnet, and when I came back I found he had given it to the hen to lay her eggs in. And you know that, only last week, when I sent him to buy a cask of butter he returned driving a hundred and fifty ducks that someone had persuaded him to take. And not one of them would lay!"

"Yes, I am afraid he is trying," replied the first, "but let us put them to the test, and see which of them is the most foolish."

So, about the time that she expected her husband home from work, the first wife got out her spinning-wheel, and sat busily

turning it, taking care not even to look up from her work when the man came in. For some minutes he stood with his mouth open watching her, and as she still remained silent, he said at last, "Have you gone mad, wife, that you sit spinning without anything on the wheel?"

"You may think that there is nothing on it," answered she, "but I can assure you that there is a large skein of wool, so fine that nobody can see it, which will be woven into a coat for you."

445

"Dear me!" he replied. "What a clever wife I have got! If you had not told me I should never have known that there was any wool on the wheel at all. But now I really do seem to see something."

The woman smiled and was silent, and after spinning busily for an hour more, she got up from her stool, and began to weave as fast as she could. At last she got up, and said to her husband, "I am too tired to finish it tonight, so I shall go to bed, and tomorrow I shall only have the cutting and stitching to do."

So the next morning she got up early, and after she had cleaned her house, and fed her chickens, and put everything in its place again, she bent over the kitchen table, and the sound of her big scissors could be heard *snip! snap!* as far as the garden. Her husband could not see anything to snip at, but then he was so stupid that this was not very surprising!

After the cutting came the sewing. The woman patted and pinned and fixed and joined. Then she turned to her husband and said, "Now it is ready for you to try on." She made him take off his coat and stand up in front of her. Then, once more, she patted and pinned and fixed and joined, and was very careful in smoothing out every wrinkle.

"It does not feel very warm," observed the man at last, when he had put up with all this patiently for a long time.

"That is because it is so fine," answered she, "you do not want it to be as thick as the rough clothes you wear every day."

He did but was ashamed to say so, and only answered, "Well, I am sure it must be beautiful since you say so, and I shall be smarter than anyone in the whole village. 'Oh, what a splendid coat!' they will exclaim when they see me walk by. But it is not everybody who has a wife as clever as mine."

Meanwhile, the other wife was not idle. As soon as her husband entered she stared at him with such a look of terror that the poor man was quite frightened.

"Why do you stare at me so? Is there anything the matter?" he asked.

"Oh! Go to bed at once," she cried. "You must be very ill indeed to look like that!"

The man was rather surprised at first, as he felt particularly well that evening, but the moment his wife spoke he became quite certain that he had something dreadful the matter with him, and grew quite pale.

"I dare say it would be the best place for me," he answered, trembling, and he asked his wife to take him upstairs and help him change into his night clothes.

"If you sleep well during the night there may be a chance for you," said she, shaking her head, as she tucked him up warmly, "but if not…"

Of course the poor man never closed an eye till the sun rose.

"How do you feel this morning?" asked the woman, coming in on tip-toe when her housework was finished.

"Oh, bad. Very bad indeed," answered he. "I have not slept for a moment. Can you think of nothing to make me better?"

"I will try everything that is possible," said the wife, who did not in the least wish her husband to die, but was determined to show that he was more foolish than the other man. "I will get some dried herbs and make you a drink, but I am very much afraid that it is too late. Why did you not tell me before?"

"I thought perhaps the pain would go off in a day or two, and besides, I did not want to make you unhappy," answered the man, who was by this time quite sure he had been suffering tortures, and had put up with them like a hero. "Of course, if I had had any idea how ill I really was, I would have spoken at once."

"Well, well, I will see what can be done," said the wife, "but talking is not good for you. Lie still and keep yourself warm."

491

All that day the man lay in bed, and whenever his wife entered the room and asked him, with a shake of the head, how he felt, he always replied that he was getting worse. At last, in the evening, she burst into tears, and when he inquired what was the matter, she sobbed out, "Oh, my poor, poor husband, are you really dead? I must go tomorrow and order your coffin."

Now, when the man heard this, a cold shiver ran through his body, and all at once he knew that he was as well as he had ever been in his life.

"Oh, no, no!" he cried. "I feel quite recovered! Indeed, I think I shall go out to work."

"You will do no such thing," replied his

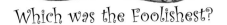

wife. "Just keep quite quiet, for before the sun rises you will be a dead man."

The man was very frightened at her words, and lay absolutely still while the undertaker came and measured him for his coffin, while his wife gave orders to the gravedigger about his grave.

That evening the coffin was sent to their home. In the morning at nine o'clock the woman dressed him in a long flannel robe, and called the undertaker's men to fasten down the lid and carry him to the grave, where all their friends were waiting for them.

Just as the body was being placed in the ground the other woman's husband came running up, dressed – as far as anyone could

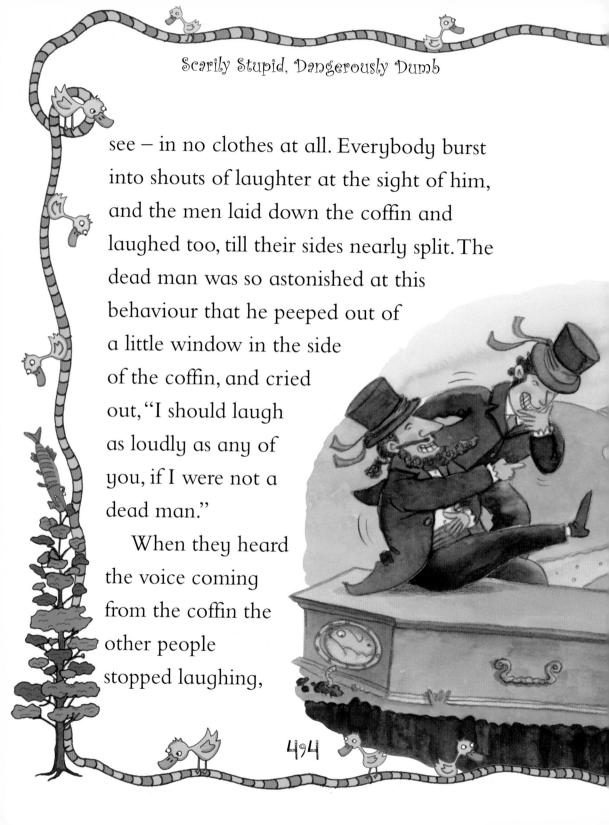

see – in no clothes at all. Everybody burst into shouts of laughter at the sight of him, and the men laid down the coffin and laughed too, till their sides nearly split. The dead man was so astonished at this behaviour that he peeped out of a little window in the side of the coffin, and cried out, "I should laugh as loudly as any of you, if I were not a dead man."

When they heard the voice coming from the coffin the other people stopped laughing, and stood as if they had been turned into stone. They rushed to the coffin and lifted the lid so that the man could step out.

"Were you really not dead after all?" asked they. "And if not, why did you let yourself be buried?"

At this the wives confessed that they had each wished to prove that her husband was stupider than the other. But the villagers declared that they could not decide which was the most foolish.

So the women quarrelled just as much as they did before, and no one ever knew whose husband was the most foolish.

The Farmer and the Money-Lender

By Joseph Jacobs

There was once a farmer who suffered much at the hands of a money-lender. Good harvests or bad, the farmer was always poor, and the money-lender was always rich. At last, when he hadn't a farthing left, the farmer went to the money-lender's house and said, "You can't squeeze water from a stone, and, as you have nothing to get from me now, you might tell me the secret of becoming rich."

"My friend," replied the money-lender knowingly, "riches come from God, or Ram – ask him."

"Thank you, I will!" replied the simple, so he prepared three cakes to last him on the journey and set out to find Ram.

First he met a priest, or Brahman, and to him he gave a cake, asking him to point out the road that leads to Ram. But the Brahman only took the cake and went on his way without a word.

Next the farmer met a holy man, or Yogi, and to him he gave a cake, without receiving any help in return.

Scarily Stupid, Dangerously Dumb

At last he came upon a poor man sitting under a tree, and finding out he was hungry the kindly Farmer gave him his last cake. The farmer sat down to rest beside him, and they entered into conversation.

"Where are you going?" asked the poor man.

"Oh, I have a long journey before me, for I am going to find Ram!" replied the farmer. "I don't suppose you could tell me which way to go?"

"Perhaps I can," said the poor man, smiling, "for *I* am Ram! What do you want of me?"

Then the farmer told him the whole story. Ram, taking pity on him, gave him a conch shell, and showed him how to blow it in a particular way, saying, "Remember! Whatever you wish for, you have only to blow the conch that way and your wish will be fulfilled. Only, be careful of that money-lender, for even magic is not proof against his devious ways!"

The farmer went back to his village rejoicing.

The money-lender noticed his high spirits at once, and said to himself, "Some good fortune must have befallen the stupid fellow to make him hold his head so joyfully." Therefore he went over to the simple farmer's house and congratulated him on his good fortune in such cunning words, pretending to have heard all about what had happened.

Before long the farmer found himself telling the whole story – all except the secret of blowing the conch, for – with all his simplicity – the farmer was not quite such a fool as to tell that.

Nevertheless, the money-lender was determined to have the conch shell by hook or by crook. So he waited for a favourable opportunity and, deviously, stole the conch from the farmer. But, after nearly bursting himself with blowing the conch shell in

every conceivable way, he
had no choice but to give
up trying. However,
being determined
to succeed,

he went back to the farmer, and said coolly,
"Look here! I've got your conch, but I can't
use it. You haven't got it, so it's clear you

can't use it either. Business is at a standstill unless we make a bargain. Now, I promise to give you back your conch and never to interfere with your using it, on one condition, which is this – whatever you get from it, I am to get double."

"Never!" cried the farmer. "That would be the old business all over again!"

"Not at all!" replied the cunning money-lender. "You will have your share! Now, don't be miserable, for if you get all you want, what can it matter to you if I am rich or poor?"

At last, though he didn't want to give the money-lender anything, the farmer was forced to give in. From that time, no matter what he gained by the power of the conch,

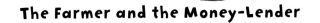

the money-lender gained double. And the knowledge that this was so preyed upon the farmer's mind day and night, so that he had no satisfaction out of anything.

At last there came a very dry season – so dry that the farmer's crops withered for want of rain. Then he blew his conch and wished for a well to water them, and lo! There was the well, but the money-lender had two! Two beautiful new wells!

This was too much for any farmer to stand, and he brooded over it and brooded over it, till at last a bright idea came into his head. The farmer seized the conch, blew it loudly, and cried out, "Oh, Ram! I wish to be blind in one eye!" And so he was, in a twinkling, but the money-lender, of course,

was blind in both, and in trying to steer his way between the two new wells he fell into one, and was drowned.

This true story shows that a farmer once got the better of a money-lender – but only by losing one of his eyes.

Laughing Eye and Weeping Eye

By Andrew Lang

Once upon a time there lived a man whose right eye always smiled and whose left eye always cried. This man had three sons – two of them were clever, and the third son was stupid.

Now, these three sons were curious about the peculiarity of their father's eyes. One day, the two eldest sons – who were afraid of their father's temper – told their simpleton brother to go and ask their father why his eyes were as they were. The simpleton did as he was told – but his father did not fly into a fury. "My favourite son," the old man said, "as you have been brave enough to ask, I will satisfy your curiosity. My right eye laughs because I am glad to have a son like you. My left eye weeps because a precious treasure has been stolen from me. I had in my garden a vine that yielded a ton of wine every hour – someone has stolen it, so I weep its loss."

The simpleton returned to his brothers and told them, and they all made up their minds to set out at once in search of the vine. They travelled together till they came to some crossroads, and there they parted –

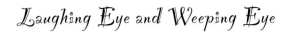

the two elder brothers took one road and they sent their simpleton brother down the other, glad to be rid of him.

After a while, the youngest son sat down and got out some food he had brought with him, and a lame fox limped out of the wood nearby. The fox asked for a crust of bread, and the simpleton gladly gave half of his meal to the hungry animal.

"Where are you going, brother?" said the fox, when he had finished his share of the bread, and the young man told him the story of his father and the wonderful vine.

"How lucky!" said the fox. "I know what has become of it. Follow me!" They went on till they came to the gate of a large garden.

"You will find here the vine that you are

seeking, but listen carefully – when you get
to it, you will find two shovels,
one of wood and the other
of iron. Be sure not to
take the iron one – it
will make a noise and
bring guards
running, and then
you are lost."

The young man
got safely through the
garden and came to the vine
that yielded a ton of wine an hour.
But he thought it would be
impossible to dig the hard earth with
only a wooden shovel, so picked up
the iron one instead. The